SING ME A MURDER

Helen Nielsen was born in Roseville, Illinois, in 1918. She worked in Chicago and Los Angeles as a free-lance commercial artist and a draftsman, as well as an aero-engineer. She began writing novels in 1951, the best-known of which are **Sing Me a Murder** and **Detour.** She lives in Southern California.

SING ME
A MURDER
HELEN NIELSEN

Black Lizard Books
Berkeley • 1988

Composition by QuadraType, San Francisco.

ISBN 0-88739-079-X
Library of Congress Catalog Card No. 87-70477

Manufactured in the United States of America.

INTRODUCTION

By Marcia Muller

In the 1950s a proliferation of male-oriented digest-sized mystery and detective magazines provided an on-the-job training ground for such writers as Evan Hunter (Ed McBain), Harry Whittington, John Jakes, and Gil Brewer. While earning a living, they also learned how to create the clean economical prose, fast-moving action scenes, and crisp dialogue that to this day are staples of good suspense writing.

Owing to the predominantly male themes and subject matter of such magazines as *Manhunt*, *Accused*, *Hunted*, *Pursuit*, and *Justice*, few of the contributors were women; but those who did break into the market were very good indeed. Of a group whose members include Craig Rice, Pat Stadley, and De Forbes (Stanton Forbes), Helen Nielsen went on to apply the exacting techniques of magazine fiction to the creation of such highly suspenseful, richly complex and critically acclaimed novels as *Detour* and *Sing Me a Murder*.

Nielsen's novels in no way fit the definition of hard-boiled or *noir* fiction as epitomized by other authors represented in the Black Lizard line (Jim Thompson and Paul Cain, for example). Her work is too emotional and we are too privy to the thoughts and feelings of her characters for the books to be classified as such. They are better termed realistic fiction: Uncompromising in their faithful depiction of the world as it is—or *could* be, had her characters actually lived and the events described by her actually occurred.

Nielsen's primary theme is that of a profound quest by her protagonist: Danny Ross, hero of *Detour*, is fleeing the United States for Mexico, not "running away from life . . . running toward it;" in the process he is forced to seek the truth about the dangerous events in which he has unwittingly become embroiled. Ty Leander, protagonist of *Sing Me a Murder*, initially appears—in his suicide attempt—to be seeking death; next we feel he is seeking to absolve another man of murder; finally his motives and aims are proven to be far more complex than either of these.

Nielsen's characters, such as Danny and Ty, are multidimensional, believably motivated, and—like most of us—not always wholly consistent. Her descriptions of them are deft—saying a great deal in few words, as in her introduction of Ty Leander:

> He was a young man, awkwardly tall. His eyes were set deep under heavy brows, his dark hair tumbled about on his head as if long uncombed by anything other than an occasional thrust of nervous fingers. His imported tweed suit nagged at his shoulders; he would always appear to be outgrowing his clothes no matter how expensive the tailoring.

This tells us all we need to know about Ty on first impression—until his puzzling actions raise questions that make us read on, seeking explanations.

The explanations are buried deep in an intricately wrought plot, and Nielsen cleverly leads us to many false conclusions before she reveals the true one. Her plots are as inventive and deceptive as any classic puzzler; we are given enough information and clues so that—however surprising the solution—we find it to be the logical conclusion of the preceding action. (This plotting ability stood Nielsen in good stead as a scriptwriter for such high quality '50s and '60s television shows as *Perry Mason*, *Alfred Hitchcock Presents*, *Alcoa Theatre*, and *87th Precinct*.) And while much of this action is violent, Nielsen neither shrinks from it nor swells upon it in unnecessary detail. Realism again. The world in which her stories take place is clearly recognizable and never sentimentalized.

Reading a Nielsen novel—in particular *Detour* or *Sing Me a Murder*—is never wholly an escape; our identification with her people; fear for their safety, and hopes for their futures is too strong for that. On the other hand, her work is always stimulating because it hones the senses and heightens our awareness of the world as we know it.

At a time when more and more women writers are receiving long overdue recognition for their realistic and hard-hitting suspense fiction, the reissue of these books is especially fitting. I, for one, am delighted to see them back in print—and I hope many new readers will discover Helen Nielsen, as I was once so fortunate to do. As respected critic Anthony Boucher said of *Sing Me a Murder*, her work is "opulent with unpredictable pleasure."

Marcia Muller
Sonoma, California
June 29, 1987

Chapter One

It was an old rooming house a few blocks behind the Ambassador Hotel. The front had asbestos shingles over the aged siding, and the porch, which stretched the entire width of the building, had been reinforced with a decorative brick trim that was now stained from time and weather. Inside the wide front door, a well-worn mahogany-railed staircase led up to the second floor. The light in the lower hall was dim, barely illuminating the lower steps; at the top of the stairs the darkness was cut only by a narrow knife of light coming from beneath the first door.

Behind the door was one man, and a voice. The music coming from the portable record player on the dresser had a deep loneliness in it, as if it had been composed by someone in search of his soul. It was an eerie kind of jazz made up of the sounds of fragmented time and old heartbeats, and in front of it—far in front, but softly—the voice of a woman singing a love chant for a passion that had come from nowhere and was going nowhere.

> ". . . the world began tonight, my love;
> the world will die tomorrow . . ."

Soft and insinuating were the sounds, and for a few moments they were the only sounds in the room except for the soft stirring of night wind at the single window, against which dangled a knotted length of rope that hung from the old-fashioned chandelier on the ceiling.

Everything was in readiness. The man stood in the center of the room and surveyed the scene he had set. He was a young man, awkwardly tall. His eyes were set deep under heavy brows; his dark hair tumbled about on his head as if long uncombed by anything other than an occasional thrust of nervous fingers. His imported tweed suit nagged at his

1

shoulders; he would always appear to be outgrowing his clothes no matter how expensive the tailoring.

He pivoted slowly. It was a small room, sparsely furnished: one bed, one lamp table holding a cheap ceramic lamp, one wall freshly papered in a flowered design matching the other walls but conspicuously new, one well-worn carpet with a bright throw rug covering an area in front of the bed, one dresser on which stood the portable record player and an unopened bottle of Scotch. Unopened. There was still one thing left to do. He moved to the dresser and went to work on the top of the bottle. He didn't have a glass; he drank from the bottle. Spill a little on the tweed jacket—neat drunks were rare. Spill a little in the flowerpot on the window ledge. The lone geranium was dying anyway, and he had to make certain that Mrs. Herbert was at her post. Faithful Mrs. Herbert. Had she seen the dangling rope yet? Nothing missed her watchful eyes. He lifted the bottle to his mouth again. The curtain at the dark window across the alleyway moved slightly. She was watching.

And Julie sang softly behind him. He drank until the warmth of the liquor began to spread through him like the warmth of Julie remembered. Julie, who could not be forgotten. Julie, who would not stay dead. A man, a voice, a bottle, and a rope dangling from the chandelier. It was time. He returned the bottle to the dresser and checked his wrist watch. Cole Riley was a very fast driver, and he would have started immediately after the telephone call. Patrolman Anderson was a methodical man; during a week of observation he hadn't failed to walk down the alleyway below on his short cut home within two minutes of the same time every night. Mrs. Herbert, who had nothing else to do with her life, was watching a lighted window from across that same alleyway.

The man returned the bottle to the dresser top and watched the arm of the record player swing back to play the record again.

> ". . . the world began tonight, my love;
> the world will die tomorrow . . ."

"Not this time, Julie," he said, softly. "Tomorrow the world begins. Act one; scene one—"

2

He loosened his tie and walked toward the dangling rope.

Coming back was like a journey through a foggy tunnel. Yellow fog. A yellow light above; three yellow faces bending over his long body sprawled awkwardly on the floor beneath the hastily cut end of rope. His legs were too long for the area between the dresser and the bed. One of them was bent at the knee and turned out, pulling up the trouser leg to show one of the bright yellow socks Julie had knitted for his birthday.

"Not yellow, Ty—saffron. Who else do you know who has saffron socks?"

"Who else do I know who has such a weirdly wonderful wife to think of saffron socks? I ask you—Cole, Alex, Marcus, have you ever heard of saffron socks?"

That memory didn't belong in the tunnel. Voices at the far end chased it away.

"He's coming around, but it was close. If that lady across the alley hadn't seen what he was doing and yelled at me . . ."

The first yellow face wore a blue cap and a blue jacket With a badge on it. Patrolman Anderson was methodical, thank God!

"It's all right, Mr. Gruenther. He's not going to die. We got here in time."

Mr. Gruenther was a paler yellow face with little sprigs of pale yellow hair jutting out from behind his ears, and bifocaled eyes with a hearing-aid attachment that glittered like a third eye under the chandelier. He carried his head sideways, as if one side of his neck were shorter than the other. He was the landlord.

"I don't like this sort of thing," he said. "Why should a man do that? Why should Mr. Tyler try to hang himself in my rooming house?"

"Mr. Tyler? Is that what he called himself?" A third voice, a third face in the yellow fog. Blond hair above the face, broad shoulders beneath handsomely encased in an alpaca topcoat that neither nagged nor crawled. Right was the word for Riley. "How long has he been living here?" he asked.

3

"A week," Gruenther said. "Not a week yet. A week tomorrow Mr. Tyler rented this place. Good-looking young man. I didn't expect any trouble. I'm getting nervous about this room. I think maybe it's got a curse."

"This room?" The fog was lifting. Now the yellow light was just a bulb in the chandelier. Beneath it, Cole Riley's face had eyes becoming aware of his surroundings. "Yes," he said, "it is the same room—"

"—where that crazy man, Flanders, killed Mary Brownlee," Gruenther added. "Officer, can't you get Mr. Tyler out of here before any of my other roomers wake up? I don't want them to think my place has a jinx."

"The same room where Mary Brownlee *was killed*," Cole corrected. "Let's not convict my client before his trial."

For a moment two pairs of eyes stared at him, the figure on the floor temporarily forgotten.

"I know you," Anderson said. "You're the society lawyer who's defending Flanders. What are you doing here? I just got here myself."

"Let's just say that I'm the lawyer who's defending Flanders," Cole suggested. "I came in right behind you, Anderson. It is Anderson, isn't it? I remember you from the Flanders hearing. I came in answer to a very dramatic telephone call informing me that the great Ty Leander was about to take his own life."

The words were caustic. They cut through what was left of the yellow fog like a knife.

"Ty Leander—?" Anderson repeated the name. "Isn't he the husband of that singer—?"

His glance darted to the dresser. Unnoticed in the excitement, the record player was still repeating the same theme. Now the music was far out—a beat, a sigh, a throaty complaint—

". . . the world will die tomorrow."

He stepped quickly to the dresser and switched off the machine. As silence came, the man on the floor stirred and uttered one recognizable word.

"Julie—"

Julie San Martin. Even the sound of her name was lovely—that had been Ty's first reaction when he heard it.

A name like music, a face like a brown-eyed angel, a body like a child turned woman. Julie with her gay laughter and the summer rain clinging in her hair.

It had been a very hot July in New York. Sensible residents left the city to make room for tourists in shirt sleeves and drip-dry nylon dresses. The streets were steaming corridors; the buildings stacks of airless cells. Eventually, all walks led to Washington Square where a quick summer shower caused paths to cross and collide—with apologies, and then with that deep stir of recognition when strangers who have been seeking one another for a lifetime know, almost without knowing, that they will never be strangers again.

At first she was just an exciting woman. Shelter from the shower was found in a coffee shop where they could begin to get acquainted. Julie San Martin, meet Ty Leander. The name means nothing to you? Wonderful! Not rich, not smart, not a celebrity-hungry Julie San Martin. A shy, uncomplicated, childlike Julie San Martin. Her address, given hesitantly when he insisted on taking her home, was in one of the Puerto Rican tenements. He couldn't leave her there. It was hours later—in the middle of the night—before he realized what the encounter had meant to him. He couldn't sleep. He'd gone to his desk and begun to write, and that was the miracle.

It had been exactly two years and four months since Marcus Anatole's roughshod playwright had burst into flame over Broadway. Praised by critics, damned by puritans, adored by a coterie of has-beens and might-have-beens, an awkward small-town boy from Indiana had been hurtled into the arms of glory, and glory is a destructive mistress. The bright flame burned high, and then, as quickly as it had risen, fell again. Marcus waited, Broadway waited, the dwindling coterie of admirers waited and then drifted away like gluttonous guests at a buffet table when the food runs out. Ty waited, wrote, destroyed what he wrote, and then turned to the bottled fount of inspiration which never inspires or eases the pain.

Alex Draeger—her credit for the sets in *Rage For Life* read Alexis Draeger—had a studio in an old stone house in the Village. Alex was one of the coterie who didn't drift away.

5

Alex and Marcus. Two friends. How many more had one the right to expect from life? Friends to comb bars, pick up a trail, track it down and somehow get him to Alex's place where he could awaken, in time, to the sick shame of living and the silent strength of Alex, a woman, a mother, a nurse. Patient, witty Alex who could mix a bicarbonate and fill an ice bag; but who couldn't bring back the flame.

And then, after two years of emptiness, suddenly there was Julie.

Within three weeks they were married, and six months later *Purple Dawn* was on the boards. Creation had begun again; the world was new. But Julie was too lovely not to attract attention of more admiring eyes than her husband's. It began at a party when she sang a few simple songs from her native country. Nothing would do but that she record a few, and that was the beginning of a wave of success that swept them from New York to Hollywood and, eventually, since Alex moved West too, into a house designed for them by Alex deep in Malibu Canyon.

It was a fabulous house. The main section—living room, kitchen, guest area—was constructed of rough wood siding, weathered and stained with the bite of salt air drifting in through the canyon. Behind the house spread a large patio laid in brick and flagstone which terminated at the edge of a shallow ravine complete with a small, sparkling stream at the bottom. Across the ravine, connected to the patio by an uncovered plank stairway, was the studio-bedroom wing built on a higher level of mountain rock. There Julie could practice in a sound-proof room and Ty could work undisturbed. By that time Julie's star was beginning to soar, and Ty had three hits behind him. Life had reached a point of perfection.

But by the morning of the 31st of October, just short of six years after their marriage, perfection had deteriorated badly. It wasn't really the Ferrari that caused the quarrel. Neglecting to have the oil changed in a $14,000 automobile was nothing unusual for Julie. It had happened before. What hadn't happened before was the coincidence of time and tension that could only end in a violent explosion of tempers. Like other wars, it had been a long time coming—the unconscious irritations, the basic wrongness felt but un-

6

definable. Julie wasn't the same any more. It was easy to blame it on her now skyrocketing success—or on Ty's masculine ego; but the wrongness, whatever it was, had upset his productivity. Marcus Anatole had come out from New York, cursing with equal vigor the smog and the sunshine, to try to prod the new play out of him; Alex was already doing sketches of the first act sets; but Ty had nothing to show for their urgings except an incomplete outline and an itching anger that finally found an outlet.

Julie had a temper, too. She could scream, she could stamp her feet, she could curse him in Spanish.

"I'm tired!" she cried. "I've been rehearsing all week and I'm exhausted. Didn't you ever forget anything when you were tired? Didn't you ever make a mistake?"

And so, because he loved her and because he was frightened at the distance between them, he shouted back at her until she ran to the closets across the room and returned with a suitcase which she began haphazardly to fill.

"I can't stand you when you're like this!" she said. "I'm going in town to stay with Alex until you get over your mood."

"Why don't you stay with Cole?" Ty taunted. "He'd love to have you as a permanent guest."

It was peculiar how ideas could pop up from the unconscious uninvited. Julie turned toward him, her face white with shock.

"Cole—?"

"He loves you," Ty said.

"*Cole?*"

She spoke the name as if she'd never heard of a man who had been their friend and attorney nearly all of their married life.

"Don't act so surprised!" Ty shouted.

"*Act? Act?* You're a fine one to accuse me! *You're* a fine one!"

"What do you mean by that?"

Julie didn't answer. She spun about and began to stuff lingerie into the bag. Hating himself, Ty helped her. He grabbed a bright blue jersey and an orange silk dress from the clothes rack and tossed them in on top of the other things.

"Go ahead!" he shouted. "Go to Alex—go to Cole! Go anywhere!"

The bright blue and the orange dresses disappeared from view as the bag snapped shut. Julie turned toward him once more, tears of fury in her eyes. She didn't speak. She took the bag and ran down the hall to the garage stairs. He didn't try to stop her. He heard the Ferrari start and then roar up the driveway and become lost in the distance. Julie was gone.

The house was empty. Ty went to his study and stared at a blank sheet of paper in the typewriter for over an hour; then, since Julie hadn't returned, wrote a note explaining that he was going to drive out on the desert to work. He packed a light bag, took the typewriter and drove off in the station wagon. Destination: anywhere that he might rent a room or a cabin without radio, television, telephone or friendly neighbors.

He drove all day to reach a motor court he'd used for such a purpose before, only to find it closed. He spent the night in the car, then turned toward the ocean and found a small lodge in the pines with a view of the shore. Perhaps it was the tempermental outburst that cleared his mind for action; he worked. He didn't think of Julie or worry about her. One night with Alex and she would have gone home again. Alex was no coddler of wounded wives.

It was about five weeks later, with the play mere pages from completion, that Ty became aware of a newscast emanating from the radio in a roadside diner. Malibu Canyon was burning—at least a score of houses already destroyed and residents streaming to the highway for safety. Within ten minutes he was in the station wagon headed for home. . . .

"Julie—"

It was hardly more than a moan, but the man in uniform caught the name. He turned back from the now silent record player.

"That's it," he said. "Julie San Martin. My wife's got three or four of her albums. If this is her husband, no wonder he wanted to kill himself." He moved closer to Cole's kneeling body and peered downward into Ty's face. "Terrible thing," he added. "I read all about it in the papers. It was that big fire in December. He'd been away somewhere and came back to find his wife burned to a cinder, and her such a beauty—" And then Anderson paused, suddenly embarrassed. "I'm sorry," he said. "I didn't think. You must have known her."

"I did," Cole admitted, "and you're right. She was a beauty."

"Ty Leander," Anderson repeated. "Why do you suppose he came here to try this?"

"I don't like it," Gruenther said. "I want you to get him out of here."

"That's a good idea," Cole agreed. "He's not hurt. Anderson, hand me that bottle of Scotch on the lamp table. Thanks. I guarantee a little of this will revive him. He's probably more drunk than injured. Now, for a little of the hair of the dog—"

Cole slipped one arm under Ty's shaggy head and put the bottle to his lips. There was marvelous recuperative power in eighty-six proof. After the first taste, Ty began to focus his eyes. The first thing they located was the rope dangling from the ceiling. The sight seemed to fascinate him. He stared at it in silence.

"I have to make a report," Anderson said. "A man can't cause all this fuss and then just walk away."

In a moment, Ty would be able to talk. "Go ahead," Cole said. "I saw a telephone in the hall—take Gruenther with you. But ask your lieutenant to keep it quiet—to keep the press away if possible. Tell him I'm here. He knows me. He'll understand."

Anderson hesitated at the door.

"We're not going to climb out of the window," Cole added. "We'll still be here when you get back."

Anderson went out. There was a snap lock on the door, and as soon as he left Cole let Ty's head slide back on the floor and went to set the lock. When he returned, the body on the floor had become revitalized. Ty had pulled himself up against the wall and was sitting up, both hands massaging his throat and his legs thrust out before him so that both saffron socks were exposed.

He looked up to find Cole staring at him.

"You're all right," Cole said bitterly. "No damage done. I don't imagine you let go of that rope until you heard Mrs. Herbert screaming for Anderson to come up here and cut you down. You remember Mrs. Herbert, don't you? She's the prosecution's prize witness against Mike Flanders. She sits glued to her window across the alley and watches the windows of this rooming house for anything juicy to gossip about. She couldn't possibly have overlooked a man hanging from a chandelier."

The color was coming back to Ty's face in splotches. He looked as if someone had rouged his cheeks. He made no attempt to answer.

"Mrs. Herbert," Cole repeated. "I told you about her last week when you came to my office. You were awfully interested in the Flanders case. Why, Ty? What's behind this elaborately staged production?"

Cole had left the bottle of Scotch on the floor. Ty's right hand reached out and found it. He raised it to his lips and swallowed, wincing with pain. When he didn't answer, Cole continued.

"You telephoned me half an hour ago. 'I'm quitting, Cole,' you said. 'I can't stand a world without Julie. I'm checking out.' Then you thoughtfully mentioned where you were so I could rush out here. You damned fool! If I'd dreamed you were actually going this far"—Cole glanced up at the dangling rope—"I'd have called the police myself."

Ty lowered the bottle slowly, his eyebrows crawling together like a pair of friendly caterpillars. Then, in a voice a little husky and edged with challenge, he asked—

"Would you, Cole?"

"That's a stupid question," Cole retorted. "You've got to stop talking like an idiot, Ty. I know how you feel. I was fond of Julie, too."

"You were in love with Julie, too," Ty said. "Everybody was in love with Julie. We never had a chance."

"Now, Ty—"

"No, don't try to stop me. It's a truth"—Ty paused long enough for one more quick drag at the bottle. This time he didn't wince—"a solemn truth," he added. "'Everybody loves a lover.' Remember that? That's an old adage. What

10

this world needs are some new adages because the old ones are obsolete. 'Everybody hates a lover'—that's how it should go. A lover destroys the status quo, and what the world loves is the status quo. Julie and I were shouting, 'Life is terrific! Life is grand!' in a mediocre, orderly age which insists in well modulated voices that life is nice. The world can't stand lust for life. It tore us to pieces."

Ty's chin dropped forward on his chest, only to come up quickly at the cut of pain. He began to massage his throat with one groping hand.

"That's a good speech," Cole said dryly, "but I always thought it was over-written. From the last act of *Purple Dawn*, isn't it? Nobody tore you to pieces, Ty. Julie died in the fire. It was horrible, and I'm sorry for you up to a certain point—but not this." He glanced at the dangling rope, his face twisted with disgust. "What you need is a session with a psychiatrist—or have you got the need for punishment out of your system?"

"Punishment?" Ty echoed.

Cole stepped across Ty's extended legs and pulled down the window shade. It was past Mrs. Herbert's bedtime. She needed a rest.

"Isn't that what it was? An act of atonement?"

Ty glared up at him. He placed his hands flat on the floor for leverage and hoisted himself to his feet. His angry face towered above Cole, until Cole grinned at him.

"At least I got you on your feet," he said.

"The trouble with you," Ty observed, "is that you're a lawyer. You don't think anyone is, or can be, honest."

"Not with that rope dangling from the chandelier," Cole admitted. "What are you trying to do, drive us all mad? You went to Marcus and told him to forget about the new play because you weren't going to write any more. You went to Alex and raved about some wild idea that Julie hadn't died in the fire after all—that the body found in the wreckage was that of someone who'd taken shelter from fire—"

Ty smiled bitterly.

"Did she really go to you with that?"

"She did. She was frantic. You told her that you were giving up everything to spend the rest of your life searching for Julie. She thought you were going out of your mind.

11

She asked me to have a talk with you, and when I did you accused me of trying to take Julie away from you. I think you're sick, Ty. I think you're really sick."

"Then why don't you have me put away?" Ty challenged. "It shouldn't be too hard to do. Everybody remembers what I was before I found Julie. Marcus Anatole's wonder boy—One-Shot Leander, with one smash under my belt and two years of nothing but clinging to the neck of a bottle. Deep emotional insecurity—ask any shrinker. All right, now my emotional security is gone. The one woman I needed to straighten me out."

For the first time, Ty seemed aware that the record had stopped playing. He turned toward the dresser and stared at the machine with somber eyes.

"But could anyone leave us alone?" he said bitterly. "Could anyone give us a chance? If I left the cap on the toothpaste and Julie complained, it was an item for the gossip mongers. If Julie had lunch with her music director and I wasn't there, we were headed for Reno. They drove us crazy. We blew up over anything—everything—nothing. Just because she forgot to have the oil changed in the Ferrari—"

"Ty," Cole urged, "you promised to stop thinking about that."

"How can I stop? I yelled at her; I screamed at her. My nerves were drum-tight and I let them break all over her. That's how we parted the day I left for the desert. That's the way it was the last time I saw her."

"But she came back to you."

"I wish she hadn't! God, how I wish she hadn't! But that's what I have to remember every time I go near that ruin of a house. And why? Because the gossip mongers tore us apart! All right, I'll give them a story! I'll give them a real story!"

There was color in Ty's face now. He saw Cole glance at the rope again and shook his head.

"No, not that," he said. "That's just the prologue before the plot unfolds. You want to know the plot, don't you? You inspired it."

Ty was talking a great deal for a man who had so recently been hanging from the chandelier. Some of it was due to

12

the Scotch; but all of it was too interesting to be ignored.

"*I* inspired it?" Cole echoed.

"Inadvertently. You were trying to get my mind off Julie. You began to tell me about the Flanders case. 'You think you have troubles,' you said. 'Here's a man fighting for his life and not much of a chance because the public already has him convicted.' 'Is he guilty?' I asked you. 'Probably,' you said, 'but I like to thwart the public blood lust whenever I can.' I liked that, Cole. I'd never known you to take this kind of a case before, but I liked that. I thought about it for days, about a man named Flanders who'd killed his girl for whatever wild reason a man like Flanders kills his girl—but who wanted to live; and then I thought about Ty Leander, who didn't."

"Ty! Don't be a melodramatic fool!" Cole protested.

"I'm not being melodramatic. I've had a month to try to get used to living without Julie—"

"A whole month!" Cole scoffed.

"—but I can't. I don't want anything any more—not anything. At least, I didn't until I thought about Flanders. Then I realized there was one thing in life that I did want."

Ty looked toward the window. The shade was drawn, but he smiled crookedly as if seeing beyond it.

"Dear Mrs. Herbert," he said. "There's always a Mrs. Herbert, isn't there? How could the world function without her? She peeks through windows; she writes columns; she even writes thoughtful, informative notes. I found a whole collection of them in Julie's room up in the stone wing of the house. . . . Why didn't she go there, I wonder? Why didn't she realize it wouldn't burn?"

Ty's questions were for himself; he didn't seem to expect an answer. But Cole had a question which demanded an answer.

"Notes?" he echoed. "What kind of notes?"

"Didn't Julie tell you?"

"Julie? No, Why should she tell me?"

"Because they were such sweet little notes—the kind a wife would take to a lawyer. No wonder a cold wind was blowing between us. 'Dear Miss San Martin, do you know where your husband really was last Thursday night when he was supposed to be at home while you were in

13

conference with your agent? Check the bar at the Ambassador.' That sort of note, Cole. A whole series of them. If I could get my hands on whoever wrote them!"

"But surely Julie knew better than to be taken in by anything like that!" Cole objected.

Then Ty looked at him, long and soberly.

"But suppose she wasn't taken in?" he asked.

"Wasn't? What do you mean?"

"Suppose her husband had been playing around. Suppose he had a girl nobody knew anything about—a pretty little waitress who lived in a rooming house behind the Ambassador."

Cole didn't answer. Words were inadequate to the bewilderment on his face.

"It's possible," Ty said. "I left for the desert on the thirty-first of October. I drove north to the motel where I usually go when I hit one of those mental blocks, but the place was closed. I spent the night in the car and cut over to the coast the next day—but the important thing is that I spent the night of the thirty-first in the car. Nobody knows where I was that night, and nobody can find out; but I could have driven back to the city. For all you know, that's what I did."

"Ty!" Cole said sharply. "What's this wild imagination of yours concocting?"

"A trade," Ty answered quietly. "That's how the law works, isn't it? A life for a life? Society demands Flanders' life when he still has use for it; but I have no use for mine. It would have been so easy when I was hanging up there to let go of that rope before Mrs. Herbert's screams brought the policeman to the door; but I was thinking of my contribution to the world. Three plays isn't much to show for thirty-six years of living. I want to really *give* something. I want to frustrate the Mrs. Herberts with their passion for retribution. They've already got Flanders strapped to the chair in the gas chamber and you're trying to cheat them by getting him off with a life sentence. I'm going to do better than that. I'm going to have a little fun before I check out of this stinking world. I'm going to see a guilty man go free."

Behind Ty's words came a new sound from the street. Cole's admonition to Anderson to keep this matter quiet hadn't carried enough weight to silence the police siren. Ty

14

smiled crookedly as a shade of comprehension began to break through Cole's bewilderment.

"Ty, you're drunk," he said. "You have to be drunk to talk this way."

The siren stopped. There was a sound of footsteps in the hall, and then Anderson pounding on the door and shouting—

"Mr. Riley? Are you all right in there, Mr. Riley?"

"Perfectly," Cole called back. "Just a moment—"

He backed toward the door, never taking his eyes from Ty's face.

"I'll tell the police, Ty," he said. "Whatever wild idea you have, it won't work. I'll tell them every word you've spoken in this room."

But Ty was still smiling. He gazed up at the rope, as if quite satisfied with the scene he'd set. He ran one hand through his hair to rumple it more and pulled his collar askew so the bruise marks would be more in evidence. Then he sat down on the edge of the bed and awaited his audience.

"Let them in," he directed, "and go ahead and tell them anything you wish. You're Flanders' lawyer; they won't believe you. But I'll make a bet with you, Cole. Just between you and me, I'd never set foot in this room until the day I rented it; but before Flanders' trial is over I'll have proven that he couldn't possibly have killed Mary Brownlee. Couldn't, you see, because she was murdered by Ty Leander."

Chapter Two

High in the hills of the Pacific Palisades, Alex Draeger's house poised like a wide-winged white gull preparing to soar over the silver ribbon of ocean that was now making an appearance through a slowly lifting veil of fog. The sun, still invisible from the glass-front living room, had touched the ribbon with shimmering light. One streak of blinding brightness under the chilly gray sky. Morning.

An Alex Draeger house—there were only four of them in existence now that Ty Leander's home stood like a charred monument in Malibu Canyon—was a poem of informality.

Alex loathed partitions. Rooms flowed into one another like tributaries to the great sea of spaciousness where four people now sat in huge, sprawling, almost formless chairs arranged in an illusion of careless disorder that can only be meticulously planned. In addition to Alex, one of the few women in the world who could look smart in a monk's-style robe worn over old-fashioned flannel pajamas, the quartet consisted of Cole Riley, sallow-eyed from the sleep he hadn't had; Marcus Anatole, who never went anywhere—even to a mysterious command-performance breakfast party—without showering, shaving, carefully combing his thinning gray hair over the growing bald spot and dressing his rotund body in the sartorial splendor that was his intercontinental trademark; and an unshaven and unsplendid young man, Dana Quist, who had answered the call by donning a soiled fisherman's sweater, blue jeans and paint-smeared canvas shoes.

Breakfast was a large enamelware pot of coffee and an electric skillet full of scrambled eggs served buffet style from the low oiled-teak slab that was the coffee table. Only Dana, piling his plate high for the second time, appeared interested in the food. The others were preoccupied with the morning paper Alex had just brought in from the front walk. Cole had been mistaken. Nobody had put a satellite into orbit or exposed a government official and so the story of Ty's suicide attempt, by virtue of his name alone, had made the headlines. The story was brief. To the small and select breakfast club Cole supplied the details.

"It took a lot of pressure to bail him out on a simple charge of drunkenness and disturbing the peace," he explained. "Luckily, Ty was his own best witness. He's upstairs now sleeping the whole thing off. I brought him here so the reporters couldn't get to him. Alex thought a conference necessary."

Marcus Anatole smothered a yawn.

"I may forgive you, Alex," he said, "someday when I'm in one of my rare good moods, although at the moment it seems an act of sheer brutality."

"Then you don't take Ty's threat seriously," Cole said.

"Of course not! Neither does Ty. It's a part of his catharsis. Let him purge himself. Let him bleed."

"You sound like a monster, Marcus," Alex said. "Ty isn't some temperamental actor on a binge. He's a sensitive man who loved his wife and lost her in a tragic disaster. I think he's sick. I think he should be stopped!"

Alex Draeger wasn't a pretty woman. At thirty-five, her features had thinned and sharpened into a classic handsomeness accented by the severe cut of her prematurely gray hair. Her eyebrows were dark and heavy and her mouth artificially generous by virtue of the lip rouge which constituted her sole concession to cosmetic art. She was tall and her frame was large. Seated, her legs stretched forward with colt-like longitude. Her strong, capable hands hung loosely over the arms of the chair. Her body appeared to be relaxed, but her body lied. The tension in her face told the truth.

Dana poured himself another cup of coffee, scrutinizing her with perceptive eyes.

"It's not like you to be so upset, Alex," he drawled. "This isn't the first time Ty's grabbed hold of a bottle for emotional security."

"But I'm fond of Ty!"

"Of course you are. You're fond of all talent, aren't you? The great and the hopeless." Dana buried his face in the coffee cup for an instant and then added—"Personally, I hope he succeeds."

"What?" Cole gasped.

"Succeeds. I'm a great believer in success. I hope Ty succeeds in proving that he killed Mary Brownlee. In the first place, his motive is excellent—cheat the public of its blood lust. Yes, by all means. This is apt to be Ty's greatest script. I never did think much of the others."

"Jealousy," Marcus observed dryly, "is the most obvious sign of impotency."

Dana glared at him across the coffee table and then buried his face in the cup again.

"I'm hoping he'll have forgotten the whole thing when he's slept off the Scotch," Cole said. "But there's one thing we can all do. We can keep tabs on Ty."

"Oh, God—yes," Alex said.

"Keep tabs on him as much as possible," Cole added, "and try to keep him from going back to what's left of that house in the canyon. He's been out there too much."

"I didn't know that," Marcus said.

"Cole's right," Alex interjected. "He's been out there brooding in Julie's room. I drove out one day intending to inspect the ruins—after all, I did design the house and I was naturally interested in how it fared the disaster. The main section was completely destroyed—nothing remains but a few blackened studs and the fireplace; but the bedroom-studio wing that I located across the patio and above the ravine is intact. It's stone—a little blackened in spots but undamaged except for the plank stairway connecting to the patio. Those canyon fires are tricky. This one destroyed the main body of the house, the patio furniture and the stairway, but it didn't jump the ravine. I didn't know what shape the driveway might be in, so I parked on the shoulder and walked down to the house. Even before I was in clear sight of the house, I could hear Julie's voice—"

"Julie's—?" Dana echoed.

"—singing," Alex added. "One of those off-beat blues things she did so well. I was startled at first—then I saw Ty's car parked in front of the garage doors and felt strange. I didn't know whether to go in or not."

"And did you?" Cole asked.

"Yes—finally. As I explained, the plank stairs to the patio are gone, but the garage is under the bedrooms and the door was unlocked. I went inside and went up the stairs Ty had taken—the music getting louder as I approached. I followed it to Julie's room. I was in the room before Ty heard me. He looked up and saw me standing in the door, and I was frightened."

"Frightened, Alex?" Cole asked. "Why?"

Alex scowled at the cup of untouched coffee held cupped in her hands. She took an apparently tasteless swallow and then added, "I don't really know, Cole. Perhaps frightened isn't the *complete* word. I felt guilty—as if I'd intruded on some altar at prayer time. Julie's voice on the record and Ty off in some other world. Oh, I've seen him in a creative trance before, but this was different. He looked disappointed—as if he'd been expecting someone else in the doorway. 'Oh,' he said, when he saw me, 'I thought you were Julie.'"

"Julie?" Dana repeated. "Ty must be off on a real drunk!"

"But he wasn't drunk; he was stone sober and serious. That's what shook me, children. As soon as I realized that I walked into the room and turned off the portable player."

"He had it with him in that room last night," Cole recalled.

"It's unhealthy, I tell you," Alex said. "I went into Julie's room that day and turned it off because I couldn't bear to hear it any more. Ever since Julie's death I haven't been able to listen to her records. Someday—perhaps. Now I just want to forget. But Ty won't even try to forget. There he was—brooding. That's why I'm so upset over what happened last night. I don't think you're right, Marcus. I think Ty is serious."

"But he can't be serious," Marcus protested. "Can't you see? If he succeeded, he'd get himself executed."

"I think that's what he wants."

"Oh, my dear!"

"I mean it! You weren't out at the house the day I walked in on him. You didn't see his face. He really *was* waiting for Julie!"

Cole hadn't touched his breakfast. He set the plate of eggs back on the coffee table and lit a cigarette. The fog was thinning. The sunlight that had made a shimmering ribbon of the sea was now a pale glow behind the soft mist.

"I've never seen Ty as the other-worldly type," he mused. "To my knowledge he's never even had a fling at Zen Buddhism let alone anything to do with spirits."

"But he wasn't waiting for a spirit," Alex insisted. "He was waiting for Julie."

A momentary silence came over the room. Three faces stared at Alex. Three puzzled, listening faces.

"Don't you see," she explained, "he hadn't accepted the fact that she was really gone? He couldn't live with the reality of her death. He started talking to me after the record stopped playing. He said that he was convinced the body that had been found in the ruins and buried as Julie wasn't really Julie at all. He'd decided that someone—some fugitive from the fire—had sought shelter in the house and been trapped in the section that burned. He insisted that Julie would have gone to the bedroom wing."

"I wondered about that myself," Marcus admitted.

"But it's so obvious that it was Julie. Her car was in the garage, her clothes in the closet"—Alex's voice stopped again. She frowned, took another drink of her coffee and continued—"and we all know how excitable she was in emergencies. I'll never forget Ty's first opening night after the marriage. I thought someone would have to lock her up. She had all of us backstage at the very edge of our nerves. No, I just can't imagine Julie thinking clearly in the fire. I'm not at all sure I would have thought of going across the ravine, and I designed the house. Furthermore, the patio furniture and the stair was destroyed; the passage may have been blocked. But in spite of all that evidence, he'd convinced himself that Julie was still alive."

"I can vouch for that," Cole remarked. "Alex came to me with the story the next day. She was scared stiff."

"I was! I really was!" Alex insisted. "I thought he needed professional care. Cole thought he could handle it by getting Ty's mind on something else. Now look at what's happened!"

"At least he is interested in something else," Dana observed. "But you mentioned that Julie's clothes were in the closet, Alex, and that reminds me of a peculiar thing Ty asked me a few days ago. Apparently he'd been talking to you and learned that we'd all gathered here for cocktails on the evening of the day he left for the desert."

"That's right," Cole said. "He asked me about that, too. He asked when was the last time I'd seen Julie alive, and that was it. I meant to call and take her out to dinner while he was gone; but within a week I was tied up in the Flanders case and time got away from me."

"Time got away from me twenty years ago," Marcus observed dryly. "The only opportunity I ever have to take a lovely lady to dinner is when her husband is out of town; but there was Julie off in that wilderness and I have a lifetime aversion to both automobiles and the feel of earth under my feet. Yes, I remember that evening, Dana. Julie wasn't herself at all. She hardly spoke to any of us."

"She'd had that silly quarrel with Ty," Alex explained. "It was nothing, actually. I knew she'd be over it in the morning."

"But she wasn't over it that night," Dana recalled. "I asked her to go to a play with me, and she didn't even answer. Not that I blame her. It was a horrid mess. But that's not what I started out to tell you. Do you remember how Julie was dressed?"

"Dressed?" Cole echoed.

"Clothes, gown, attire?"

"I'm afraid I don't," Cole admitted.

"The legal mind," Marcus observed, "sees only faces and emotions. But Dana is an artist. You remember, don't you, Dana?"

Dana ignored the trace of condescension in Marcus' voice.

"She was wearing an orange silk," he said, "that flaming orange that was so striking with her dark hair. I told Ty. 'I thought so,' he said. 'It had to be the orange or the—'"

Dana's voice stopped mid-sentence. He was facing the stairway—a wide spiral design composed of thick slab treads that seemed to hang in space until one noticed the fine steel network that held them in position. The treads led up to a loft area, off which opened four slab doors. One door now stood open, and Ty, arrayed in one of Alex's terrycloth pool robes, had come out to the head of the stairs. He might have been there for some time. He remained motionless until all eyes, following Dana's direction, located him; then he descended slowly. His hair was uncombed and an overnight growth of dark beard shadowed his face. He said nothing. He looked at each of the four faces in the room and then walked over to the coffee table. He lifted the top from the enamel pot, sniffed the contents and shuddered. He replaced the lid of the pot and made his way to a low sideboard across the room. From the, sideboard, he removed a bottle of cognac, uncorked it and drank deeply. Then he turned and stared at Dana.

"You didn't finish your story," he said. "'It had to be the orange or the blue'—that's what Ty said to Dana. 'It had to be the orange or the blue.' Good morning, Alex. Your robe fits me beautifully, if you don't mind my bony ankles. Good morning, Marcus—Cole—Dana. Good morning, one and all."

So saying, Ty took another long drink from the bottle.

"Oh, I'm sorry," he said. "I forgot there are ladies present—correction, a lady. Forgive me if my slip is showing. Cole's right. I had enough last night."

He re-corked the bottle and returned it to the sideboard. He stood against it a moment, looking suddenly lonely and sad.

"I'm not very beautiful, am I?" he said. "And this darned belt—"

"Oh, Ty—"

Alex left her Chair and cane across the room. The belt of the robe was dangling. She pulled it together and did the knot. When she looked up, he was smiling shyly.

"I guess I need a woman's touch," he said.

He walked over to the windows and stared out at the ocean. It was a cold, glimmering gray. The fog had thickened again momentarily.

"It might rain," Ty said.

"I don't think it will," Cole remarked.

"But it might." Ty turned about and faced them, both hands in the pockets of his robe. "Julie," he said. "Alex knew what was happening before I did. Don't you remember, Alex? It was one day at your studio—about two weeks after I'd found Julie. She asked me if I ever wore brown. She said I'd look good in brown, and Alex said, 'Be careful, Ty. When a man mentally undresses a woman it's merely sex; but when a woman mentally dresses a man he's in dire danger of matrimony.' We were married a week later."

Cole glanced at his wrist watch and stood up.

"This is all very interesting," he said, "but I think you'd better get back to bed, Ty. I've got to be going. I've only a few hours before court convenes."

"Court? The Flanders case? Wait for me. I'll get dressed." Ty moved quickly toward the stairs.

"No—you're not going down to that courtroom," Cole ordered. "You've caused enough sensation already."

Cole motioned to the morning paper Alex had tossed onto the coffee table. The headline brought a wry smile to Ty's face.

"Good notice," he said.

"Ty, this isn't amusing," Marcus insisted. "It's a bad joke. A very bad joke."

Marcus never wasted words. His admonition was serious. Ty hesitated at the foot of the stairs, one hand idly finding the head of a Mexican stone lion Alex had set in place of a newel post. Four faces were watching him, and each of the four mirrored disapproval.

"All right," he said, "forget it. I was drunk. It was just a wild idea."

Four faces still watched him.

"It certainly was," Cole said at last.

"I'd like to go to the trial anyway."

"But the reporters—" Alex broke in.

"I won't let them see me. I'll just be a spectator. It's something to do."

"You could get back to work," Marcus suggested.

"Not today. Some other time. Wait for me, Cole."

Ty ran up the stairs. There was no stopping him. Five minutes later he returned, dressed and rubbing his chin with an exploratory hand.

"I'll grab a shave somewhere," he said. "Thanks for the hospitality, Alex." He leaned forward and kissed her lightly on the cheek. "And my apologies to everybody for routing you out at an ungodly hour. You should have known better. You should all realize how Ty Leander works off his emotional problems."

For a moment Ty was almost gay, and then he reached into his coat pocket and withdrew two bright objects to hold in the palm of his hand.

"Dana," he said, "what color are these?"

"Why, they're ear clips," Dana said. "Emeralds."

"And Emeralds are green," Ty added. "They were Julie's. They were found on her body after the fire."

And then he turned abruptly to Cole.

"Ready?" he asked.

Chapter Three

The story of Mary Brownlee was a familiar one. There wasn't a soul in Judge Henderson's court, including Ty, who hadn't read the details of her violent death. A very pretty girl, according to the news photos, dark hair and eyes, slender—almost girlish—body. A waitress who had lived alone in a rooming house; a girl who would naturally be popular with men, and, unfortunately, jealously loved by one.

That one was Michael Flanders, a brick-topped giant of thirty-eight, neither handsome nor unhandsome, his somewhat blunt features having a slightly swollen appearance of sensuality. At least, so the press and the public perceived them. It was a sordid story of a brutal crime, brightened by the gaudy finery of a holiday celebration.

"She sure looked fancy. She was wearing one of those Gay Nineties outfits, all spangles and a real tight waist. You know—"

The old man on the witness stand was Herman Gruenther, tense and miserable in his unaccustomed limelight. Standing before him, Felix Washburn, District Attorney, questioned and drew forth answers with long-practiced skill. Now he walked to the exhibit table and returned with an armful of red-and-gold satin.

"Is this the costume, Mr. Gruenther?" he asked.

The old man adjusted his glasses and leaned forward. A few seconds of consideration and then—

"Yes, sir. That's the costume. I'd stepped outside, you see, to put out a bowl of candy on a card table on the porch. I always do that on Halloween. Saves running to the door every time some kid comes for trick or treat. I seen Mary coming down the stairs on my way back inside. I whistled at her—in fun, you know. She had a coat thrown over her shoulders, but it wasn't fastened. She was on her way out."

"Did you ask her where she was going?" Washburn queried.

"Didn't have to ask," Gruenther said. "She told me she was waiting for her boyfriend to take her to a party. I went back inside my apartment and about ten minutes later I heard a car drive up and honk and she went out. I never did see her alive again."

The Halloween Party Murder. It was the kind of case the headline writers loved. Mary Brownlee had gone to a costume party with her boyfriend. She'd been seen there, masked but recognizable—chiefly because of a loud and conspicuous quarrel that had taken place early in the evening. Mary had walked out. Her date, also masked, had followed. Two days later . . .

The story everybody knew continued to unfold; and the fact that everybody knew it did nothing to dull the interest.

"Saturday was the first of the month," Gruenther was saying. "I try to keep a strict rule that all my roomers pay the rent on the first. That's the only way to run a place. Be easy with one and the first thing you know nobody pays."

"But the day you found the body, Mr. Gruenther . . ." Washburn prodded.

The old man was warming up to his brief glory. He seemed reluctant to let it end.

"That's what I was getting around to," Gruenther said. "I didn't see Mary on Saturday. I figured she was at work, as usual. Thursday is her day off, not Saturday. I thought she'd stop by and pay me when she came home. When she didn't, and then didn't even come down Sunday morning, I went up to her room and rapped on the door. It began to open—oh, I'd say about four or five inches. Enough for me to see inside and notice something lying on the floor."

Gruenther spoke slowly, his words rambling and slightly hoarse. The courtroom had become very still. From his seat in the rear of the spectators' gallery, Ty was hardly aware of the disturbance beside him until he heard a familiar voice, softly, at his shoulder.

"How is it playing?" Marcus asked. "The house looks good."

Ty, frowning, turned toward him.

"What are you doing here?" he demanded.

"Keeping tabs," Marcus answered.

"What?"

25

"Keeping tabs on Ty. That was Cole's directive shortly before you came down this morning. To be more explicit, you're under surveillance. Dana couldn't come; he had to go elsewhere today. I was drafted."

A middle-aged feminine face under an elderly cloche turned about and glared at Marcus from the row just ahead, her lips pursed in an indignant "Shhh—!"

"A charming ghoul," he murmured to Ty. "Probably covering the trial for the next meeting of the Mothers' Club."

". . . acid," Gruenther had said. "I knew it was acid burns even before the medical examiner came. Some of it had spilled on the floor and on the wall. I had to repaper and buy a throw rug. It was terrible—even her eyebrows gone. And to think that she'd been there like that since Friday night without my knowing."

"Then you didn't see or hear her return that night?" Washburn asked.

The old man turned his head and pointed to the hearing attachment on his eyeglasses.

"I go to bed at ten o'clock every night," he explained, "and when I do, I take this contraption off. If there's any fussing or fighting in the house after ten, I don't lose any sleep over it."

Marcus was restless. He hated crowds of any kind—even paying crowds.

"Why do you want to stay here?" he asked. "Why can't you get back to work and forget this nonsense?"

"It isn't nonsense," Ty retorted. "This is the real thing, Marcus. A man is likely to die—"

From the witness stand, Herman Gruenther was now explaining a previous reference to violence in the house. It was a particularly damaging piece of evidence concerning quarrels between Mary Brownlee and her boyfriend.

"Once I heard something smash on the floor, so I ran up to her room to see what was going on. I heard him tell Mary to stay away from other guys or he'd fix her face so she wouldn't look pretty again. . . ."

Marcus leaned closer.

"Let him die," he said. "Anyone who would disfigure a beautiful woman deserves death."

"Cole doesn't think so," Ty remarked.

26

Cole sat beside Flanders, impressively calm in the face of Gruenther's testimony. Flanders seemed bewildered, as if not fully aware of the significance of the whole affair. It was time for District Attorney Washburn to make the point he'd been carefully building up to all this time. Stepping aside in order to clear Gruenther's view, he said, "Mr. Gruenther, I want you to make a careful search of the courtroom and tell me if you see Mary Brownlee's boyfriend—the one you heard threaten to disfigure her face if she went out with another man."

Gruenther strained forward, his eyes owlish behind thick-lensed glasses.

"Yes sir, I do," he said, at last. "He's sitting right over there beside that lawyer. It was him—Michael Flanders."

There was a stir in the courtroom as everybody shifted position in order to get a better look at the defendant. Now Flanders seemed embarrassed and confused. He turned toward Cole like a small boy looking for his mother in a crowd.

"Why am I under surveillance?" Ty asked Marcus.

"After that ridiculous stunt you pulled last night," Marcus answered, "how can you ask? That wasn't like you, Ty. You've never been a publicity hound."

"I was drunk," Ty said.

"So I heard—"

There was something challenging in Marcus' words. Ty glanced at him. His usually unperturbed face wore a slight frown; his eyes were studying Ty carefully.

And from the front of the room, Cole Riley was beginning the cross-examination of Herman Gruenther. Cole was careful, poised, a man in command. He was inquiring whether or not Mary Brownlee was habitually late with her rent. He was drawing out small bits and pieces of the portrait of a dead woman. She was fond of nice clothes—sometimes she overspent on them and could only make a token payment until more money came in.

"Until her next payday, you mean?" Cole asked.

"Until more money came in," Gruenther said. "I never asked where it came from. I suppose she borrowed from friends. She sure liked nice things."

A gaudy party costume displayed on the exhibit table,

and the portrait of small human frailties painted by an old man's words, were making a dead woman begin to live. She was young, she was beautiful, she liked being admired, she wasn't at all practical . . .

". . . I can't remember everything," Julie had said. "I looked at the speedometer only a week ago and it wasn't time for an oil change."

"A week ago!" Ty scoffed. "You've driven that car four hundred miles since the last change time. Do you drive four hundred miles in a week?"

"All right—two weeks ago! I forgot! Didn't you ever forget anything?"

Ty was staring straight ahead, no hint of his thoughts mirrored on his face.

"Why did he kill her?" he asked aloud.

"Flanders?" Marcus shrugged. "Who can say? One wrong word at the wrong time. Something trivial, probably."

"Like the oil change," Ty mused. "She had it changed after all. Did you know that, Marcus? I found the new sticker on the door, and I got the bill about ten days ago."

Marcus continued to study Ty's face, still staring at the scene before them.

"Who are you talking about?" he demanded.

Ty didn't answer.

". . . Mary Brownlee," Cole was recapitulating, "was overly fond of nice things and frequently spent more than she should for them. She was an attractive young woman who, apparently, had more than one admirer. Isn't that so, Mr. Gruenther?"

While Gruenther hesitated over the question, the district attorney objected to the wording. Cole replied with a polite exposition of his reasoning: if the defendant had threatened to disfigure Mary's face if she went out with other men, it was reasonable to suppose that she knew other men. Gruenther had already admitted that she must have friends, because she seemed to get money from sources other than her paychecks. . . .

"The eye of the hurricane," Ty said.

"Now what are you talking about?" Marcus asked.

"Hatred," Ty said. "There's a hatred beyond fear; a ha-

28

tred beyond love. There's the eye of the hurricane in us all, the quiet place where the storm ceases end the only reality left is the one thought—kill. We all kill, in one way or another, those who refuse to love us."

"Ty," Marcus said softly, "you should be home—working."

"I want to watch Cole operate," Ty answered. "It's time for him to make his point."

Cole's timing was perfect.

"On Halloween night," he said, "on the night when you saw Miss Brownlee in costume and she told you that she was waiting for her boyfriend to take her to a party, did she name her date of the evening, Mr. Gruenther?"

The old man adjusted his glasses and fidgeted in the chair.

"No, sir," he said at last.

"And later, when you heard a car drive up to the house and honk for her, did you look out of the window?"

"No, sir," Gruenther said.

"And you didn't hear or see her return?"

"No, I'd gone to bed—"

"Then you can't actually identify the man with whom Miss Brownlee went out on the night of the murder, can you, Mr. Gruenther?"

Gruenther seemed puzzled by the question.

"It was him—" He started to point at the defendant as he had previously done under Washburn's questioning, but now his hand fell back on his knee in anticipation of Cole's next question.

"Did you actually *see* the man Miss Brownlee dated the night of the murder?" Cole demanded.

The old man's head lowered.

"No, sir," he admitted.

"Thank you, Mr. Gruenther. No more questions."

Cole turned away from the stand, a faint smile of confidence on his face; but the smile was to fade before he could resume his place beside Flanders. Gruenther had been dismissed, but he wasn't finished testifying.

"Maybe I didn't see him," he shouted at Cole's back, "but I know it better had been him!"

The words were unexpected; the language puzzling. Cole turned and hesitated an instant too long.

29

"It better had been him," the old man repeated, "because if she went out with another man he was going to fix her face for her—and that's just what happened!"

Cole's triumph vanished. He stood rooted to the floor, his poise a relic of habit. Herman Gruenther left the stand, the sudden object of news photographers' cameras. A witness, not either of the counsels, had drawn first blood. Judge Henderson rapped for order as the bulbs began to flash. Marcus yanked on Ty's arm.

"Let's get out of here," he said. "I think that redheaded one has recognized you."

Marcus was already in the aisle. Ty came slowly to his feet. For a few seconds he towered above the rest of the spectators like a tousled giant facing the battery of photographers.

"Ty Leander—"

He'd been seen. Marcus dragged him into the aisle and toward the doors to the hall, the furious banging of the judge's gavel a lost gesture behind the excitement of the new discovery; but not before Ty caught one vivid glimpse of Cole's face—white with fury.

"What you don't seem to understand," Cole said harshly, "is that a murder trial is a serious procedure—not a sideshow. I warned you against coming to court after that wild suicide attempt last night; I was afraid you would be recognized. But no, you were going to sit quietly in the back of the room and just watch. When I saw you, you were standing there like a scarecrow. Why didn't you wave your arms? Why didn't you yell, 'Here I am, boys! Come and interview me'?"

Time had passed; Cole's anger hadn't. The disturbance caused by the dual events of the landlord's unsolicited testimony, together with that of the discovery of an illustrious visitor among the spectators, had resulted in a recess until after lunch. Not wanting to be molested by the press, Cole had returned to his office—catching Ty and Marcus in the parking lot to which they had fled. Lunch was a sack-and-carton affair sent up from the lunchroom on the first floor.

"There's no great harm done," Marcus said quietly.

"No harm done? I'm upset—that's harm enough. I need all my wits about me if I'm going to do Flanders any good."

Ty wasn't hungry. He'd taken a carton of coffee and strolled over to the typewriter on the secretary's desk. He sat down and inserted a sheet of paper into the machine.

"You slipped up on the landlord," he remarked, tapping the machine with one finger. "I was surprised, Cole. I didn't think you would leave yourself open that way."

Cole glared at him.

"Perhaps I wouldn't have left myself open if I hadn't been up all night with a drunken friend."

"Please," Marcus scolded, "don't bandy words. If you want to fight, hire an arena."

"I don't want to fight," Cole said. "I just want Ty to amuse himself in some other manner. I've got an almost impossible job ahead of me. I'd counted heavily on scoring on Gruenther's testimony, because all I can build a case on is the possibility that Mary Brownlee was keeping company with another man, and that he, not Flanders, killed her. Nobody saw him at the rooming house that night. Mrs. Herbert from across the alley heard a violent quarrel in Mary's room on the previous night and will testify that she saw Flanders through the window. But on the night of the murder she seems to have been strangely deaf. She's upset about it, too. The one time something worth eavesdropping on occurred she missed the whole show."

"Dear Mrs. Herbert," Ty said. "Then there's no problem."

"No problem!" Cole pushed back his chair and came to his feet. "This afternoon, or possibly tomorrow, Washburn is going to call to the stand a teller at Mary Brownlee's bank who will testify that she closed out her checking account of over five hundred dollars on the day of her death. No money was found in her room; but when Flanders was picked up in Las Vegas a week later, he had nearly three hundred dollars on him and no explanation of how he'd come by it—he's been living on unemployment insurance for the past three months—other than a story about a poker game he says he was in at the time the murder was committed, which is to say at some time after ten o'clock on the night Mary Brownlee went to the party. If it had been prior to ten o'clock, the old man downstairs would have had his hearing aid on and picked up the disturbance."

"If there was a disturbance," Ty mused.

Cole glanced at him quizzically. He seemed about to speak but Marcus interfered.

"Who was in the poker game?" he asked.

"Flanders doesn't know. Apparently it was one of those games that go on more or less continuously. He doesn't even remember where it was. He just says that he went there with somebody named 'Cappy.' He doesn't seem to have known the last name."

"A big help," Marcus said.

"Oh, great! What about it, Ty? Any bright ideas as to how I'm going to convince a jury that Flanders didn't get his money from a woman he'd just killed?"

Ty pushed back his chair and stood up.

"He won it in a poker game," he said bluntly.

Then he turned and, apparently oblivious of the two pair of troubled eyes watching him, walked to the door.

"Wait for me," Marcus called, struggling in his chair.

Ty looked back, smiling.

"I'll be a good boy," he promised. "No riotous behavior."

The door closed behind him and he was gone. Marcus settled back in his chair.

"I think you should follow him," Cole said. "I don't like the way he's talking."

"I don't like it either," Marcus admitted, "but following him just now isn't good. I want to talk to you. I don't understand this, Cole. A woman. What can a woman do to a man to make him like that?"

"Julie?"

Marcus nodded, his face suddenly very tired.

"He was talking about her back there in the courtroom. You were describing Mary Brownlee and he asked me—"

Marcus cut off his own words in silence.

"What did he ask you?" Cole demanded.

Marcus shook his head.

"That's the trouble; I'm not sure. He seemed to get the two women confused—Mary Brownlee and Julie. Do you know, I'm beginning to think that Alex may be right. Ty may not be well."

"What did he say in the courtroom?" Cole persisted.

"I don't remember all of it—something about the eye of the hurricane. I don't know. I couldn't be sure which woman he had reference to. Did he ever say anything to you about Julie getting"—Marcus paused, his face disgusted at the thought—"the oil changed?"

"He talked about it last night," Cole said. "Julie had neglected to have her car serviced at the proper time; that's what sparked their quarrel the day she walked out on him and he decided to go to the desert."

Marcus nodded. "That explains it," he said. "A part of it." And then he stared up at Cole with troubled eyes. "Ty *was* drunk last night, wasn't he?"

Cole had moved over to the secretary's desk recently vacated by Ty. His eyes dropped to the sheet of paper in the typewriter, and then one hand reached out to remove the sheet and crumple it.

"He'd been drinking," he answered.

"But he couldn't have been serious about what he said!"

"I don't think so," Cole said. "I don't think any man could really be serious about a thing like that."

"Any man—no. Ty Leander—who knows? Oh, I've nursed Ty a long time—long before you met him, Cole. I know how erratic he can be. Sometimes he's a prophet on a mountaintop, and again he's like a child playing with blocks too large for him to lift. That's why the public goes to see his plays. They can identify—especially with the child and the blocks. But now, without Julie . . ."

Cole still held the crumpled paper in his left hand.

"You weren't particularly concerned this morning," he reminded.

Marcus nodded gravely.

"Catharsis," he repeated. "Something he had to work out of his system. But a little while ago in that courtroom—Cole, I think I know how Alex felt when she found him in the ruin of the house waiting for Julie. Tell me, just what *did* Ty say last night? Did he give any specific reason for wanting to prove himself guilty for Flanders' crime?"

"Specific?" Cole echoed.

"Anything. Anything at all."

Cole moved back to his desk. The gesture was underlined with impatience.

"Marcus," he said, "I don't like to be rude; but I've got a rough afternoon facing me."

33

"Of course," Marcus said. "I'm sorry. We'll have a talk later." He struggled to his feet, brushing a few crumbs from his brass-buttoned vest. "A woman," he mused. "How can it be? How can a woman do for a man what Julie did for Ty, and how can her death do to him what it's done?"

"Have you never been in love?" Cole asked.

"Love?" Marcus echoed. "What is love? A form of egotism. Ty's lost a mirror he was fond of gazing into to admire his own reflection."

"Julie—a mirror?"

"Ty's mirror—yes."

"And that's all she was?"

There was a tinge of something close to anger in Cole's words. Marcus looked up, surprised.

"Now, don't take offense," he said. "We're two bachelors, but we're not children."

"But I thought that Julie was a human being. I thought she was an individual with a life and a soul—or are we too adult to think in terms of soul?"

Now Marcus was amazed and hurt. He stared at Cole's face for a moment. It had a kind of arrogance in anger.

"I think I'd better leave now," he said. "I'm getting you upset and doing nothing for Ty. Maybe we can make sense of this later when you haven't so much on your mind."

Marcus left the office, and only after he was gone did Cole unfold the crumpled paper in his hand. Ty hadn't completed his typing exercise, but the text was familiar.

Dear Miss San Martin,
  Do you know where your husband really was last Thursday night when he was supposed to be in conference . . . ?

Chapter Four

The Ferrari was painted luminous bronze—a hard-top coupé with beige leather upholstery and dashboard. It was small and slender, and Julie had fitted into it as if it had been molded to her measurements. Ty had to adjust the driver's seat as far as it would go whenever he drove the Ferrari, and even so he felt as if he were sitting on the back of his neck.

The Ferrari had 11,480 miles on the speedometer. On the morning of October 31st, it had registered 11,402. The oil should have been changed at 11,000; it was changed, according to the sticker on the door, at 11,440. In spite of such lapses of care, the automobile was in top condition; and Ty would have appreciated having it handy when he emerged from Cole's office in the sharp, slanting rain. But the Ferrari was parked where he had found it on his return from his writing hideaway—in the garage under the undamaged wing of the Malibu Canyon house. Ty hailed a cab and drove westward.

The asbestos shingles of the rooming house took on the color of wet cardboard in the rain. Ty paid the cab driver and hurried to the door. He still had the key and let himself in. He was halfway up the stairs before a voice from below arrested his progress.

"Hey, you there—"

Ty stopped and turned about. Herman Gruenther hadn't been delayed with lunch in Cole's office. He'd scurried home again where he would be safe from questioning attorneys and blinding flashbulbs. The glory would be for future reminiscence. At the moment he was just an irritated landlord bent on protecting his property.

"What are you doing here?" he demanded. "Ain't you caused enough trouble?"

"I live here," Ty said quietly.

"After what happened last night? I don't want that kind of roomer in my place. You didn't even give me your right name. I read all about you in the morning paper."

"You'll read about me in the evening paper, too," Ty said.

Gruenther edged closer to the staircase, his eyes straining to see. Only one bulb lighted the lower hall, and it was a small one.

"Why, you were in the courtroom this morning," he said. "What are you up to, anyway?"

"I just wanted to hear your testimony, Mr. Gruenther," Ty said. "You did a fine job up on the stand. Most people are so nervous about testifying in court that they let the attorneys twist and turn them any way they wish. Nothing like that happened to you."

The flattering words had the desired effect. Gruenther's forbidding attitude softened.

"I told the truth, like I was supposed to," he said. "An honest man's got nothing to fear from telling the truth."

"That's right, he hasn't," Ty admitted. "This Mary Brownlee, now, she must have been quite a number."

Wariness crept into Gruenther's eyes.

"I'm not one for prying," he said. "I've always tried to run a respectable place."

"But you allowed her to take Flanders up to her room," Ty protested.

"Allowed? I never allowed! I can't watch this stairway all the time, and my hearing ain't what it should be even with this contraption. He got up there, all right; but I never allowed!"

"What about her other callers?" Ty asked.

"Others?"

"Didn't you ever see anyone? What about the day of the murder?"

"Mary Brownlee worked daytimes."

"But didn't she ever come home on her lunch hour?"

"Why should she? She was a waitress. Lunch was part of her pay."

"Still, she might have come home anyway. I know I would if I lived so close to my work. I'd have things to do— telephoning, an appointment, a delivery—"

If he tried every possibility, Ty might hit on one thing that would arouse the old man's memory. He had succeeded. Gruenther's face, until now wry with disdain, suddenly brightened.

"Oh, you mean the package," he said. "I'd forgotten about that. It did come that day."

"Package?" Ty echoed.

"Don't know what was in it. Never even saw who delivered it. I'd just stepped out into the hall about noon and I saw this big package going up the top of the stairs. What I mean," he added, noting Ty's puzzled expression, "is that the package was all I did see. Somebody was holding it at the top so it hung down—a long package, like a suit box. I couldn't see anything else because there's not much light gets up there."

"How do you know the package was for Mary Brownlee?" Ty asked.

"Because I heard whoever it was that brought it knock on her door. I was going to yell up that nobody was home; but before I could, the door opened and I heard Mary say 'Oh, you brought it with you,' and then the door closed. I went back inside my place then and stayed there." The old man paused, frowning over his story. "Do you think I should have told those lawyers that?"

"Did they ask you?" Ty said.

"No, I guess that's right. But look here, young fellow, this talk don't change nothing. I still don't like you coming back here—"

Gruenther's voice stopped as the front door opened and someone came into the hall. Without looking around, Ty leaned against the railing in order to make passage for whatever tenant would be coming up the stairs; but the large, raincoated figure who stepped in under the small arc of light was no one he'd previously seen on the premises. There was something professional about him, as if he were accustomed to entering houses where he didn't belong. He looked up at Ty on the stairway. His face was partially shadowed by the moist brim on his felt hat; but his eyes were alive and knowing. They left Ty momentarily and returned to the landlord.

"You got out of that courtroom awfully fast, Mr. Gruenther," he said. "I didn't have a chance to talk to you."

"I wanted to go home," Gruenther said. "I don't like that place."

"I don't blame you. A courtroom isn't a good place to be during a murder trial. Some of us, being witnesses, have to be there; but I've always wondered why people who don't have to be present insist on coming."

The question had no specific direction; but the man's sharp eyes had turned toward Ty again.

"My name is Janus, Lieutenant—Homicide," he said. "I know Mr. Gruenther because I came here the day Mary

37

Brownlee's body was discovered; but I don't believe we've met, Mr. Leander."

Ty wasn't quite sure what the proper reaction should be when a police officer introduces himself. He said nothing.

"He calls himself Tyler," Gruenther interposed. "He took that room up there a little more than a week ago. He said then that his name was Leroy Tyler."

"Now, that's interesting," Janus mused. "Why did you do that, Mr. Leander?"

Ty hadn't moved from his position on the stairs. The lieutenant's voice was neither challenging nor sarcastic. He was just a polite policeman waiting for an answer to his question.

"I frequently do things like that," he said. "I like to hole in somewhere when I work."

"Don't you have a place to work at home, Mr. Leander?"

"My home burned down in the Malibu Canyon fire last month," Ty said.

Janus nodded sympathetically.

"Yes, I remember that. Lost your wife, too. I'm sorry, Mr. Leander."

The words must have been interpreted as a dismissal by the landlord. He'd been easing back toward the door of his own apartment. Now he stopped.

"I don't like him staying here," he objected. "I don't like anybody that goes around trying to hang himself."

Ty smiled tightly.

"I don't make a practice of that," he said. "Last night I felt low, and I'd been drinking."

"So I've heard," Janus remarked. "Don't you think that room up there could have had something to do with your mood? It has a morbid association."

"I wanted the atmosphere," Ty said.

"Oh? Doing research on the Brownlee murder?"

"Why not? It's an interesting case."

"Yes, it is." Janus withdrew a package of peppermint wafers and offered the package to Ty. When Ty refused, he offered it to Gruenther, who carefully picked off the top wafer and dropped it into his mouth. "Wife's orders," Janus said, taking the next wafer for himself. "'Too much smoking,' she said. She's right, too. That's the trouble with having a nagging wife, they're nearly always right. Did your wife nag, Mr. Leander?"

Lieutenant Janus was a quiet, deliberate man. It was obvious by this time that it wasn't Mr. Gruenther he'd come to see. These thoughts passed quickly through Ty's mind as he stood there on the stairway, one hand on the worn railing.

"No, she didn't," Ty said.

"Never? You were a lucky man."

"I always thought so," Ty admitted.

"And she was such a beautiful woman, too. Yes, you really were lucky. you probably never thought of looking at another woman."

"I've *thought* of a lot of things," Ty said.

Janus grinned. He had quite a pleasant face when one became accustomed to being scrutinized by a policeman. He'd forgotten all about Gruenther, who had backed against the door of his apartment, his mouth working on the peppermint and his eyes, magnified behind his bifocals, watching both men with unconcealed curiosity.

"Then I guess a great playwright is as normal as anyone," Janus observed. "Still, I can't help thinking it would be better to stay away from that room upstairs."

"Why?" Ty challenged. "Is it haunted?"

"The room?" Janus shook his head. "Rooms are never haunted, Mr. Leander—only people."

"He plays those records," Gruenther broke in, like a small echo from the rear. "That dead singer's records." The old man seemed uncertain of the identity of the singer he was objecting to, as well as her relationship to the roomer on the stairs. But he did object. "Like to drove me crazy," he added. "He was worse than Mary Brownlee. She did the same thing. Sometimes I'd have to turn off my hearing aid long before ten—"

"Mary Brownlee?" Ty interrupted. "Did she play Julie's records?"

"Julie's?" Gruenther seemed puzzled. "I don't know whose records they were. I figured they were hers."

"The singer," Ty explained. "Julie San Martin. Did she play the same records I played?"

39

Gruenther shook his head. "They sounded the same," he said, "but I couldn't really say. All this new music sounds the same to me. Somebody bangs some kettles, and somebody else blows a horn, and some female moans. . . . Lieutenant, do I have to put up with a roomer in my house who plays records at all hours and then tries to hang himself? And about that drinking. I don't allow drinking in the rooms in my house. If you want to drink, go out to a saloon; but I found a bottle up in that room last night. Now, I want this man to get out of here."

"I've paid my rent for a month in advance," Ty said. "Do you want to refund it?"

The old man lowered his head. He didn't answer. He looked hopefully at Janus and received no help.

"I can't put Mr. Leander out if he wants to stay," Janus advised. "I can only appeal to his common sense. After what happened here last night, anyone else would be under observation in the psycho ward. But this is Ty Leander, and his lawyer friend, Mr. Riley, took care of everything for him. I have to warn you, Mr. Leander, he won't be able to take care of anything if something like that happens again."

"Do you think I've come back to finish the job?" Ty queried.

"I don't have any idea why you've come back here," Janus admitted. "I don't even know why you came here in the first place. I understand that sensitive people do peculiar things at times, and at times they don't even know why they're doing them. That reminds me—"

Janus reached inside his coat pocket and withdrew a small white envelope. From it he took a folded sheet of white linen tablet paper, which he proceeded to unfold and then hand over to Ty.

"Have you ever seen this before, Mr. Leander?" he asked.

The message was printed in an uneven, blurred type. It read—

Dear Miss San Martin,
    Your husband didn't keep his dinner date Thursday night, did he? It's a shame that you don't know the reason. She's quite lovely.

Ty refolded the note and handed it back to Janus.

"Trash," he said angrily. "That sort of thing happens all the time to people in my"—he paused—"and Julie's position."

"But haven't you seen it before?" Janus persisted.

"Why should I?" Ty challenged.

"I thought that your wife might have shown it to you?"

"She wouldn't have given it a second thought!"

The face of Lieutenant Janus was grave and slightly puzzled. He turned the envelope over in his hands. Ty could see the address—in the same blurred type—and the canceled stamp.

"If she didn't give it a second thought," he mused, "I wonder how it came to be sent to me. U.S. mail—first class. Just a week ago." Janus looked up and held Ty with his eyes. "But you don't know anything about that, I suppose."

"Nothing," Ty said.

"Still, you must admit that it looks peculiar. The letter was sent to your wife and now I have it. Somebody must have been going through your wife's belongings."

"That's possible," Ty said. "A great many people were going through what's left of our house only a few weeks ago—firemen, insurance adjustors, friends. People are always taking souvenirs from a celebrity's home."

"A strange souvenir," Janus said, pocketing the letter.

"Maybe somebody wants to get me into trouble," Ty suggested.

Janus shook his head knowingly.

"An amateur," he said. "Judging from what happened here last night and what happened in the courtroom this morning, I'd say you don't need any help in that department. Still, it's darned strange that the letter was sent to me. I don't usually get fan mail. Of course, I did have my picture in the paper a couple of months ago when I brought Flanders back from Las Vegas."

"Sorry I missed it," Ty said. "I was out of town. Now, if you don't mind, I'd like to change my shirt."

Lieutenant Janus backed away from the stairway.

"Go right ahead," he responded, "but don't let your necktie get too tight—and, Mr. Leander"—he glanced

41

at Gruenther who still stood against the door of his rooms—
"no records."

Ty went up to the room at the head of the stairs. Before
he reached the upper hall, he heard Janus go out through
the front door. He'd been right in his suspicion; the police
officer hadn't come to see Herman Gruenther. Ty took out
his key and let himself into the room. The rain made the
afternoon seem farther spent than it was; the room was
shadowed and dreary. The only brightness in it came from
the one wall where Gruenther had covered the acid holes
with fresh paper of a matching design and the throw rug on
the floor which hid the burns in the old carpet. The record
player and the records were still on the dresser; but the bottle of Scotch was nowhere in sight.

"Enjoy yourself, Mr. Gruenther," Ty mused aloud. "Life
has few pleasures."

Mrs. Herbert was getting hers. Across the alley way, the
sound of a television newscast blared out details of the
day's progress of the Flanders trial. Ty moved to the window, open a few inches, and shoved the sash up as far as it
would go. The wind caught the ends of the net curtains and
waved them like twin banners in the rain. Gruenther
would have more to complain about.

". . . the landlord of the rooming house in which Mary
Brownlee met her tragic death, described a scene of
horror . . ."

The newscaster sounded as if he were on the verge of a
nervous breakdown. Gruenther's hesitant monotone was a
distinct anticlimax.

". . . acid. I knew it was acid burns even before the medical examiner came. Some of it had spilled on the floor and
on the wall. I had to repaper . . ."

The paper had clusters of small flowers—roses, probably.
Weren't roses the usual thing to put on wallpaper? Small
flowers linked together with loops of ribbon—silver and
pink on a background turning yellow with age except for
that one conspicuous wall.

". . . I go to bed every night at ten o'clock. When I do, I
take this contraption off . . ."

Ten o'clock on Halloween night. Friday. Date night. The

42

walls in the rooms of this old house were thicker than in newer buildings, and Mary Brownlee's room had a huge walk-in closet separating it from the next room. She'd left the party early—few of the roomers would have been in, or, if they were in, would have been listening to radios or television sets. Murder was possible in such a house. But what about Mrs. Herbert?

". . . Gruenther was followed to the stand in the afternoon by Medical Examiner Tobias, who testified that death was caused by one of the numerous blows on the back and side of the head, and not by the disfiguring acid thrown on the victim's face after death . . ."

Blows. Ty turned his back to the window and studied the room. After a week, he was familiar with it. The dresser was of hardwood. His hand tested the sharp edge of one corner. A fatal blow might be possible here. The bed had only a headboard of cheap plywood padded with plastic; but the frame was of steel and a sharp edge jutted out beyond the mattress causing the spread to wear thin at the point of protusion. Fatality was possible here. But again, what of Mrs. Herbert? She'd heard a quarrel on the night previous; but not on the night of the murder.

"Probably out on her broomstick," Ty muttered aloud.

The voice of the newscaster was gone, and a nauseating child began to demand that mother buy a certain brand of toothpaste. Ty stepped over to the dresser to get what he'd come back for—a clean shirt out of the top drawer. While changing, he could look down and see Julie's face gazing up at him from the cover of her last album. She was watching him with those wide dark eyes that never seemed to be able to decide whether to smile or to cry. They had always been the eyes of a child—hurt and bewildered, and yet ready to forgive at the slightest sign of acceptance. Could they be gone forever? Could anything so alive be dead?

He finished buttoning the shirt and reached for a necktie.

"Not the gray one, darling. Why do men always want to look so drab? Don't you know that a woman wants her man bright as a peacock?"

Julie. Ty dropped the neckwear and looked up. His own startled face stared back at him from the mirror behind the dresser—his face, the new paper on the reflected wall, the throw rug on the floor. Nothing else. The door to the hall was still closed, and there was nothing else to be seen. Lieutenant Janus was right; rooms weren't haunted—only people. And yet he waited for more words to come, as if they were important and in a moment Julie would tell him why. He remembered a room and faces: Julie, Alex, Marcus, Cole. But what room, and why should it come to mind because he held a dull gray necktie in his hand? It wasn't this room, certainly. A gay room filled with bright, gay people. But wasn't there something about a too gay party that sent a message seeping through the pores—*false, false, false?*

"Who?" he asked plaintively. "Who, Julie?"

But she was only a paper face on the cover of a record album. She couldn't tell him the answer. He waited and then put down the gray tie and took up a brown and gold foulard. By this time, Mrs. Herbert's television was silent. He slipped back into his jacket and returned to the window. The tails of the curtains hung limp and wet now, and below, in the parking area at the rear of the building, the top of the station wagon had attained a glossy sheen. He glanced up. Mrs. Herbert's face, round and sharp-eyed, was peering at him from across the separating alleyway. He reached up to pull the knot of the tie tighter, and then, remembering Janus' parting admonition, jerked the tie upward and let his head drop in an exaggerated imitation of a man dangling from a noose. He smiled wryly as Mrs. Herbert scurried out of sight.

When Ty went downstairs, Mr. Gruenther's door was closed and the hall was empty. He descended slowly, measuring each step with his eyes. At the bottom of the stairway stood a ceramic pot intended for planting, but used as an umbrella holder. Gruenther's long-handled black umbrella was in it. No one was in sight. Ty went out unnoticed, took the station wagon, left in the parking area because of Cole's intervention on the previous night, and drove around the corner to an independent service station. A dark-haired attendant in coveralls was busy resetting one of the automatic pumps. He finished the task, came around to the driver's side of the car, and grinned broadly.

"Why, hello there, Mr. Leander," he said. "Say, didn't I read something about you in this morning's paper?"

"Hi, Nick," Ty responded. "I guess I really hung one on."

"Yeah—in more ways than one! Don't you know guys get killed fooling around with ropes like that?" And then Nick's face stopped kidding and became grave. "You've got to stop taking it so hard, Mr. Leander," he added. "How come you're over in this neighborhood, anyway?"

"Fill up the tank with special, Nick," Ty ordered.

The request stopped conversation for a few minutes; but when Nick returned and began to clean off the windshield, he was still loquacious.

"Still got the Ferrari, Mr. Leander?" he asked.

"Yes, I've still got it," Ty answered.

"Sure is a lot of automobile! You know, I never serviced a car like that before. Worked on a Mercedes-Benz once; but never a Ferrari. I really got a thrill out of it."

"It's a nice car," Ty admitted.

"Nice? Say, like I told you before, a car like that one I never forget. Check the oil, Mr. Leander?"

"The oil's okay," Ty said. "Nick—"

Nick had started off to the cash box to write up the service ticket. At the sound of his name, he hesitated.

"Has anyone else been in here asking questions about the Ferrari?"

"Anyone else? No—nobody."

"Somebody will," Ty said. "When that happens, be sure you tell everything just the way you told it to me."

Nick was thoroughly puzzled. He considered the request for a few seconds and then, without further comment—

"Got your credit card, Mr. Leander?"

Ty handed him the card and watched him go to the cash box at the end of the pump island to write up the ticket. It would be done in duplicate, the carbon to be retained by the customer. Julie never quite understood about that.

"I want you to keep the tickets, Julie. I know it seems foolish to you, but that's how I balance our account each month. Don't throw them out of the car window, and don't wad them up in your purse. Keep the tickets, Julie—please."

And Julie had become angry, which was her defense against having made a mistake.

"All right, I'll keep them. I'll save each one. I'll press them out if they get wrinkled in my purse. I'll put them in a little pile here

in my desk drawer so you'll always know where to find each precious one!"

That had been Julie's promise; but, like many of her trivial promises, she had forgotten. One receipt—the last one with the address of Nick's station on it—had been carelessly dropped to the floor of the car. Ty watched Nick until he was almost ready to return for the customer's signature, and then shoved the station wagon in gear and nosed it into the street.

"Mr. Leander—hey!"

Ty didn't look back. In a matter of seconds, he was caught up in the traffic and Nick was left staring blankly at the empty driveway.

Chapter Five

Sometimes the wind blew along with the rain—blew in wild off the ocean, like a god angered at the clutter of houses spoiling the natural beauty of the hills. Prodding, insinuating, bending all vegetation before it, the strong fingers of the wind worried at the windows and gnawed at the sliding glass doors of the white house in the Palisades. Between the house and the wind was nothing but the tight clutch of the anchoring beams clawing deep into the sandstone shale; and between the house and the howl of the wind was nothing but walls and glass.

"I always feel as if I were on the deck of a ship caught in a high gale when the wind blows up here, Alex. I need a ration of grog to weather the storm."

"I hate the wind," Alex said.

Alex's voice was quiet and hard. Marcus turned from the windows to scrutinize the expression on her face.

"Yes," he said. "That's true, isn't it? You've always hated the wind. I remember one summer on Nantucket—"

"Never mind that now," Alex ordered. "We're discussing Ty. What did he say, Marcus? What did he actually *say?*"

It was late afternoon. Marcus had come back to Alex's house with a troubled mind. Now he groped for words to tell a story he didn't understand.

"What he actually said is nothing," he answered. "It's what he's *not* saying. He plants seeds, Alex."

"Seeds?"

"Suggestions. I think he's doing it deliberately."

The sky and the sea were a cold, depressing gray. On the opposite wall, warm flames beckoned from the long, low gash that formed the fireplace. Marcus moved toward it.

"If there's to be no grog," he complained, "I must get my warmth from a more primitive source."

"Oh, hush!" Alex said. "I'll get you some grog. Whisky? Brandy?—"

"From the lush Caribbean islands of—"

Marcus got no farther. "Bourbon!" Alex announced, returning glass in hand. "Drink it or perish of thirst."

Marcus took the glass, grimacing.

"I must confess, Alex, I can't understand you," he said. "A sophisticated woman of the world—afraid of wind and fond of bourbon. It's incomprehensible."

"Ty," Alex repeated, seating herself on a low hassock in front of the fire. "Concentrate, Marcus. We were discussing Ty and what he said to you in the courtroom."

Marcus swallowed deeply of the bourbon and eased gently into one of the wide chairs.

"I had something else in mind when I came here," he said.

"In particular?"

"Julie. Julie's last words."

"Last words? How should I know that?"

"Because you were the last to see her—of our little group, I mean. Think back, Alex. Did you see Julie or speak to her by telephone after she left your house on—when? The day after our cocktail party?"

The fire licked hungrily at the logs in the fireplace, the wind an appetizer overhead. Alex folded her narrow-trousered legs along the sides of the hassock and hunched forward like a child listening to a story.

"Yes," she said quietly.

"November first," Marcus mused. "Forgive my accuracy, but I've been all morning in a courtroom where details are constantly underscored. So Julie went home the next day. Morning or afternoon?"

Alex hesitated.

"We had breakfast," she said, "and talked. It was more like brunch, I suppose. Is it important?"

"In a courtroom, very important, and what I'm trying to do is hold a sort of informal court over what's troubling Ty. I want to fix the last time any of us saw Julie alive."

"But why—?"

"I'll tell you shortly. Now, did you happen to telephone Julie at any time after that date?"

Alex grew thoughtful. She was puzzled, but curious enough to co-operate.

"No, I'm afraid I didn't," she confessed. "I meant to, but I'm not much for telephoning and I've been awfully busy. I've a new commission for a house, and the sets for Ty's play, and, of course, Dana out in the studio. Besides, Julie promised she was going to stay home and relax—no work, no engagements, just help Ty with the play. She didn't know he was gone, of course. She couldn't have found out until she got home."

"And she didn't call you then?"

"Why should she? Ty told us later that he left a note. Julie wasn't a neurotic, afraid to stay alone. She only came in to me that day because she was angry. You know her temper." And then Alex paused, measuring Marcus' face with shrewd eyes. "Marcus, what's on your mind?" she demanded.

Marcus stared past her into the fire, as if the flames might give him the answer he didn't know.

"I'm afraid Ty has them mixed up," he said.

"Mixed up? Who?"

"Julie and Mary Brownlee. Don't you see, it's the coincidence of the dates. Mary Brownlee was murdered on Halloween night. Julie left here the next morning. I'm afraid the shock of coming home to find her dead, coupled with Cole's involvement in the Flanders' case, has caused some confusion in his mind."

Such a statement required clarification. Carefully, Marcus recreated the scene in the courtroom when Ty accompanied the examination of Gruenther with his cryptic dialogue. Carefully, Alex listened.

"This could be what's really behind his threat to convict

himself of Flanders' crime," Marcus added. "If he imagines there's some connection between the two events—"

"That's ridiculous!" Alex protested. "If Ty thought that Flanders had killed Julie, he'd want him to die."

"Flanders kill Julie?" Marcus echoed. "What a thought! That's not what I had in mind at all."

"Then what did you have in mind?"

"The story you told us this morning, Alex. You said that you found Ty in the studio of the Malibu Canyon house waiting for Julie. He says he's given up the idea that she's alive—at least he told Cole as much—but has he? What about the orange and the blue dresses? And what about the emerald earclips?"

The fire blazed high, casting a red glow on Alex's face. She was more than puzzled now; she was worried.

"I've been wondering about that all day," she confessed. "I even tried to discuss it with Dana; but he's in one of his enigmatic moods. He suggested that Ty is playing up the tragedy of Julie's death for sympathy; but that's not Ty—you know that!"

"Not for sympathy," Marcus agreed. "Self-flagellation, perhaps. Ty's been torturing himself ever since I met him; but we've got to stop this before it goes any further. Cole was furious. The mess last night with the headlines this morning, and then getting caught in the courtroom today. We shouldn't have let him go, although how anyone can ever stop Ty Leander from doing what he's set on doing is beyond me. This thing could get out of hand, Alex. That's why I want to know about Julie."

"Her last words?" Alex recalled. "Why—?"

"A figure of speech. What I really want is to find someone who saw her after she left here on the first. It was—what? Five weeks before the fire."

"That long?" Alex reflected. "Yes, you're right."

"Then someone must have seen her. The house is isolated; but isn't there a village?"

Alex didn't answer; but she watched Marcus' face intently.

"I seem to remember a village," he said. "You drove me out one Sunday—over my protests. We drove through a village or some kind of shopping center." Then Marcus' face

49

brightened. "And stopped at a filling station," he added. "That's it, Alex. That's where we'll find out about Julie. She had the oil changed."

"The oil changed?" Alex repeated.

"Ty said so. Apparently it has some significance which hasn't been explained to me. He said that Julie had the oil changed after all. He found the sticker on the door and received the bill."

Alex stood up. Marcus looked at her expectantly.

"Shall we go out there now?"

She stared over his head at the windows fronting on the sea. The wind could be heard; not seen. Nothing was movable on that horizon except the clouds, and they were lost behind the skein of incoming fog.

"It's rotten weather," she said.

"Still, if we could help Ty."

"The oil changed—"

"Is it important?"

"They quarreled over it. It wasn't really important, but I suppose there's only one way to find out if Ty had any ulterior motive in mentioning it. I'll get my coat."

Alex's garage was on a lower level, a two-car area with ample space for storage. A stack of old sets, a discarded drafting table, and several unidentifiable objects covered by a canvas tarpaulin were stacked at one end of the space; Alex's Lincoln was at the other. As they pulled away, the drive switched back to meet the street at the rear of the house, passing on the way a long, low building with a huge skylight in the shed-type roof. It was located about two hundred feet behind the house—a separate unit with its own garage fronting on the street. The garage doors were open, disclosing an empty interior.

"Dana's taken some textiles he designed and dyed to a show in Pasadena," Alex remarked as the Lincoln nosed into the street. "He's quite promising—"

"He's a parasite," Marcus said abruptly. "Young, handsome and charming, when he's not being a deliberate snob, but a complete parasite. Why do you do it, Alex? Why do you collect these young men? They always despise you."

"Once upon a time I 'collected,' as you put it, Ty Leander.

50

He wasn't a parasite, and I don't think he's ever despised me."

"Lightning seldom strikes twice in the same place, Alex."

"I can hope."

The road curved down an incline somewhat precarious in the soft rain that had now slickened the pavement. Alex drove carefully, her eyes fixed on the road ahead. Marcus watched her profile, his own face creased with a slight frown.

"You should have held on to Ty," he said.

"Held on—?" Alex echoed.

"You discovered him. You brought him to me. 'Marcus, I've got a fortune for you,' you said. He was all yours then."

"Don't be foolish!" Alex protested. "I never wanted Ty for myself. I wanted his success. I'm not possessive."

"No," Marcus admitted, "you're not that at all. You're a very generous woman, Alex."

The words were complimentary; they merely sounded cold. Alex stopped at the signal at the Pacific Coast Highway and glanced at Marcus' face; but Marcus could be as enigmatic as an Easter Island image. The signal changed and she headed the Lincoln north.

It was raining harder, and continued to rain harder until they were well inland from the canyon cut-off. Alex drove carefully; conversation died. Better than halfway through the canyon, she turned off at an intersection and continued to a small cluster of buildings—a general store, a post office, a filling station. The rain was lighter now, but the wind was still wild. Alex parked the Lincoln beyond the pump area and, accompanied by Marcus, made her way to the station office. Inside, a lean, raw-boned young man, wearing a leather jacket over his khaki shirt and trousers, sat behind a flat-topped desk working over a ledger. He looked up at their entrance, glanced toward the pumps and, seeing no vehicle awaiting service, eased back in his chair.

"Something I can do for you?" he asked.

Alex was the spokesman.

"We're friends of Mr. Leander," she said. "I take it that you know him."

"Mr. Leander?" The man pushed back his chair and came to his feet. "I sure do," he said. Then his face sobered. "I haven't seen him for a week or more. Say, I hope there's nothing wrong."

He waited for reassurance. Marcus found a high stool near a portable electric heater and made himself as comfortable as possible under the circumstances. Alex turned the conversation to Julie. As she did so, the man's expression changed from consternation to bewilderment.

"Did I see Mrs. Leander any time during the five weeks while her husband was away—is that what you want to know?" he asked.

"That's what I want to know," Alex said.

"Now, that's peculiar. It's the very same thing Mr. Leander asked me—oh, two, three weeks ago."

"Mr. Leander," Marcus echoed. "Did he come to you asking about his wife?"

"He sure did. He seemed surprised when I told him I hadn't seen her in all that time. To be honest with you, I was surprised, too. Mrs. Leander used to put on a couple of hundred miles a week. By rights, she should have been in here two or three times during that period."

"And she wasn't in at all?" Alex asked.

"Not at all. I even asked Sam—he's my relief man—but Sam hadn't seen her."

"Then she didn't get the oil changed here," Marcus observed.

He glanced at Alex. Her face was taut and strained. A gust of wind caught an empty oil can and sent it clattering across the paved driveway between the pumps. Alex pulled her coat collar tighter. The station man, catching Marcus' remark, shook his head and smiled crookedly.

"Now, there we are again," he said. "That's just what Mr. Leander said. He told me the oil had been changed in the Ferrari because he'd seen the sticker on the door. I was curious. 'Whereabouts?' I asked. 'On the opening side or on the hinge side?' 'On the opening side,' he said. 'Then I didn't do the job, Mr. Leander,' I told him. 'I always service Mr. Leander's car myself—won't let Sam touch it—and I always put the sticker on the hinge side of the body, not on the door at all.'"

Alex had been listening intently.

"What did Mr. Leander say then?" she asked.

"Not much. Not much at all, but he was upset. I could see that, all right. I can't blame him. I really feel bad about Mrs. Leander. Everybody around here did. You know, it's a peculiar thing, but I thought of her several times while Mr. Leander was away. I didn't see her come down to the store, and I didn't see the car. I even thought of driving up past the house to see if she was sick; but then, a person never actually does anything like that. We just think about it and then get busy and forget."

"You knew, then, that Mr. Leander was away?" Alex queried.

"Oh, sure. I knew that. He stopped by to have the station wagon tanked up the morning he left. He was really in a black mood that day. 'Orin,' he said—that's my name, Orin Peters, right up on that sign outside—'Orin, you're a single man. Stay smart. Never marry.'"

"Mr. Leander and his wife had a little argument that morning," Marcus advised.

Orin Peters nodded. "That's what I figured. Still, I was surprised. A man with a woman like that for a wife—well, you know what I mean. I told him. I said, 'You say a thing like that with a wife like yours? She's a real living doll!' And then he said a thing I've never forgotten."

The sound of a motor on the highway took Peters' attention away from his callers momentarily. The vehicle slowed at the intersection, but didn't turn in at the pumps. Peters turned back to find two pairs of interested eyes fastened on him.

"I'll bet Mr. Leander hasn't forgotten it either," he added, "but things like that happen. I had a hunting dog once—a beagle hound. Best hunting dog I ever had. I really loved that dog. Some people can't understand how it is to love a dog. They think you're a little peculiar—you know. Well, not a real man. A real man learns to love his dog."

"What did Mr. Leander say?" Alex asked.

Peters ignored the interruption. "But she was a moody bitch," he added. "Aggravating, you know? Out on the field there wasn't a finer dog afoot; but around the station she was a darned nuisance—underfoot, always in the way. One day, after I'd stumbled over her for about the sixteenth time, I said to her, 'Why don't you move out on the

53

highway if you want to stop traffic?' It didn't mean anything, what I said, but darned if ten minutes later she didn't take after a squirrel and get herself run over and killed by a truck. I was sick, I tell you. I cried. I cried like I saw Mr. Leander crying the day he got back and learned that his house had burned down with his wife inside it. It does something to you. It's crazy foolishness, I know, but it makes you feel guilty. That's why I've never forgotten what Mr. Leander said that morning when I told him his wife was a living doll. I hope he's forgotten. 'Dolls,' he said, 'are pretty to look at and to play with, but, believe me, they shouldn't be living.' I sure hope he's forgotten."

Driving home, Alex tied to find words for what both she and Marcus were feeling.

"He was upset that morning. You know Ty. His temper's murderous when he's striving for a creation that won't come."

It was almost dark and the rain heavier along the coast. Marcus watched the wiper fanning out across the windshield before him for some seconds before he answered.

"And yet, Peters is right," he mused. "The quarrel troubles Ty. If he made such a remark, he certainly feels guilty."

"That's primitive nonsense," Alex protested.

"Is the primitive nonsensical?" Marcus reflected. "Are we so far removed from our origins as that? We're all primitives —Ty in particular. He's little more than savage at times—so am I, if you will believe me. So"—he paused and studied Alex's grim profile for an instant—"are you."

"But that remark meant nothing!"

"Except for the moment he said it. The eye of the hurricane."

"What?"

"The expression was Ty's. I'm beginning to understand it. With the right coincidence of time and opportunity, who on earth wouldn't be a murderer?"

"You're not saying that Ty—?" Alex couldn't take her eyes away from the road; she could tighten her grip on the steering wheel. "Exactly what," she asked, "is on your mind, Marcus?"

"Motivation," Marcus said. "A man doesn't even joke

54

about the sort of thing Ty told Cole last night unless he's seriously depressed. I think Ty feels guilty for Julie's death, Alex. I think that's why he refused at first to believe she'd died in the fire—it was a kind of self-protection. Don't you see what's happened? No one saw her—she apparently didn't even go shopping for five weeks."

"Didn't you ever notice the size of Julie's food locker?" Alex protested. "Alone, she could have lived for months without going out. And I know from my own experience that five weeks can pass like a weekend if I'm busy or just relaxing by myself. There's nothing sinister in none of us seeing or hearing from Julie in five weeks. Just think—how many similar periods have there been when the same thing happened?"

"True," Marcus admitted, "but with one difference. At the end of those periods, Julie was still alive. This time she wasn't. That's why he's apt to let his imagination get away from him. If no one saw Julie during those five weeks, then perhaps she didn't go back to the house."

"But the Ferrari—" Alex protested.

"Please, patience, Alex. I'm trying to reconstruct Ty's reasoning. He wanted her to be alive; not only because he misses her, but because if she were alive he'd not be guilty of her death."

"Oh, Marcus, you're talking nonsense! Ty's not trying to make himself not guilty; he's trying to make himself guilty—of Mary Brownlee's death."

"I wonder . . ." Marcus said.

They had reached the turn-off to Alex's house. For a few moments the road took all of her attention. As the first sharp curve eased into the broad rise toward the crest, she asked—

"What do you mean?"

"I wonder," Marcus repeated, "where Julie had the oil changed."

There was no opportunity to pursue the subject farther. They had reached the crest and swung into the flat approach to Alex's property. The garage doors at the studio still stood open; but now an aging Ford convertible was nosed in at the entrance, parked at an angle that partially blocked the driveway to Alex's house. She braked to a stop and touched the horn. Once, twice—

"Honestly, Dana is so thoughtless!"

Alex opened the door and prepared to step into the street, and then, in front of the headlights that were poking through the slant of rain into the dark garage, a figure appeared—disheveled and stumbling with one arm thrown up over his forehead as if to shield his eyes against the light. When the arm lowered, Marcus spoke the obvious—

"It's Dana. Look, Alex, he's bleeding!"

Chapter Six

When Ty left Nick's service station on Eighth Street, he drove north to Wilshire and then turned west. It was a long drive to where he was going, and he had much to think about on the way. The day had been interesting. Both Cole and Herman Gruenther had told him things of great importance. By this time, the elderly landlord's victory on the witness stand had crowded his own escapade of the previous night off the front pages. At every corner newsstand along the way he could glimpse the headline story of the first blood drawn in Flanders' murder trial. At one red light, he beckoned the newsboy to the window and bought a copy. Traffic wouldn't allow reading time; but he could at least study Flanders' face in the front-page photograph, caught in that moment of Gruenther's accusation—not shocked, not frightened, not even angry; but acutely self-conscious and vaguely aware that something significant was occurring and that it was unfavorable to his case.

Michael Flanders was a man to be studied. His brief history was summed up journalistically as "unemployed dry cleaner" or "part-time cleaner and dyer." The inference was clear. Michael Flanders wasn't a citizen of substance or means; he was spasmodically employed at a job which gave him knowledge of and access to various bleaches, dyes and other acids: chemicals capable of disfiguration. The association was easy to make. Clumsy, lumbering, obviously not overly bright, Flanders would have been warned by his employers to be careful of acids and combustible materials. He might have spilled some on his hand and remembered.

Mary Brownlee was a beautiful girl, her beauty would have been the high point of her vanity. Destroying that beauty to keep her from attracting other men didn't make much sense after she was dead; but it would make perfect sense to an infuriated lover who wanted to wipe out the very memory of the face of a woman who had tormented him. And Michael Flanders, who seldom worked, had money when he was picked up in Las Vegas. Obviously, he must have taken it from Mary Brownlee. If she'd given him money at other times, didn't the pattern fit? It would have made Flanders a kind of vulgar gigolo, and gigolos always despised the women who kept them. Disfiguration was their favorite form of retaliation when they were dismissed.

Yes, Ty reflected, Cole had a real job on his hands if he thought he could save Michael Flanders from the death cell. It was a good thing that his reputation was established; it couldn't be hurt by defeat. But then, Cole wasn't going to be defeated. . . .

It was a very long drive. Ty reached the turn-off to Alex's hilltop house just as a long Lincoln nosed out onto the highway and headed north. Alex's Lincoln, easily recognizable at so short a distance. Alex and Marcus. Ty hesitated at the turn. They hadn't seen him, obviously. Where would they be going in this weather if not to the house in the canyon? It was a great temptation not to follow them; but with Alex gone, and a fragment of Marcus' courtroom conversation lodged in his mind, it was time to finish what he'd come to do and pay a call on Dana Quist.

Dana. Ty's face wore a tight scowl as the station wagon roared up the incline. Dana was one of Alex's young men. An artist, a composer, a struggling playwright—always there was someone that Alex carried under her wing. Alex, the protector of genius—except that all she had to show for her trouble thus far was one quite a bit less than genius playwright who had lost everything in life that gave him reason to go on working. At the top of the grade, he swung toward the studio where Dana's garage still stood open and empty. Marcus had said Dana was spending the day elsewhere—that was what Ty counted on. Even if Alex had been at home, her house was far enough away to allow him the freedom he needed to accomplish what he'd come to do. Housebreaking was illegal; but streets so high in the hills weren't patrolled. However, just in the event that he needed to get away fast for any reason, Ty drove past the garage, turned the station wagon about, and parked a hundred feet distant from the open garage.

He walked back, the rain slanting in sharply from the ocean that churned sullenly beneath the heavy sky—wide, bleak patches of it visible between the trees. No rain could reach inside the garage; but there was an almost deliberate clutter about the place which left only a small area, marked by crankcase drippings, in which Dana could park his aging Ford. Dana was as disorderly as Alex was orderly. Her garage was as neat as her living room; Dana's had to be trekked through like an expedition into hostile territory. Amid the clutter of bottles, cans, and other loose debris, Ty's foot kicked up a capped glass jar containing a few nails and sent it rolling across the floor. He retrieved it, emptied it, stuffed it into his raincoat pocket. He walked on to the connecting door to the studio and, finding it unlocked, entered. Dana never locked doors. Dana had nothing anyone would want to steal—ordinarily; but Ty had come on a particular quest.

The interior of the studio was as disorderly as the garage, except that there was more room for the clutter and a few pieces of furniture—chiefly low, comfortable couches—upon which to heap it. It was one long room, the northern half of the shed roof given over to a huge skylight—the only window in the room—with a bar-type kitchen, a Pullman bath, and a series of deep closets at one end. In between, against the wall opposite the window, was a long work table and a sink with storage cabinets above for art and drafting materials. Once this had been Alex's workroom with a place for everything and everything in its place; now it was Dana's and one had to search.

It was an angry room. Ty became aware of that after he'd stepped on a cushion that could only have been thrown from the couch across the room and discovered a pile of sketches ripped and scattered on the floor. Impatient anger? Dana was young, barely twenty-four, and yet, at times, he had such control as to execute the series of textile designs Ty uncovered amid the clutter, so fine in detail as to make the careless mess around him seem impossible. He kicked the flame-colored cushion out of his path and continued the search. Finally, there was a cupboard bordering on neatness—a series of glass containers bearing the labels of chemicals used in Dana's work: "Hydrocyanide," "Acetone," "Nitric Acid"—no need to look farther. Ty pulled the glass jar from his pocket, uncapped it and set it in the zinc-lined sink. He then took the jar of acid and carefully transferred just enough of it into the smaller container to moisten the bottom thoroughly. He then recapped the small jar and replaced it in his pocket.

Mission accomplished. Now there was silence, except for the rain washing down the skylight—rain and a blanket of gray overhead. Ty picked up the flame colored cushion and kneaded it in his hands. He was an intruder in another man's home; he should leave before Dana returned. But there was still something that needed doing while he was here. He walked slowly about the room, searching among the clutter for something that might not be there. Did Dana Quist possess a typewriter? If so, it must be hidden. One thing was found which was familiar enough—a record player with the record in place. Ty read the label:

> Julie San Martin . . . So Dead My Love ". . . the world began tonight my love; the world will die tomorrow . . ."

Ty stopped the record almost as soon as it had begun to play. He looked among Dana's collection of records and albums that were scattered on the floor near the player—Julie San Martin, Julie San Martin—

"Dana, too," he said aloud. Dana, Cole—how many more? Everybody loved Julie, except someone who sent letters.

"If I'm ever murdered—"

Houses couldn't talk—not even unoccupied studios; and yet the words were as clear as if they had been spoken. It was the past talking—a poignant fragment of something almost remembered. Ty stood in the center of the room, clutching the flame-colored pillow in his hand and trying to clutch with his mind the rest of the words. Where had they come from? It was that moment in Mary Brownlee's room all over again, the room that couldn't be haunted. But he

59

was. It was as if Julie were trying to tell him something. What connection could there be between a gray tie and the words that had just come to him?

"Julie—?"

He spoke her name aloud. It made her seem more real in his mind. But there had been so many Julies. Call one and another would answer.

Julie ran toward him, laughing. There was no rain; there was sunshine on the beach, and she dropped down beside him to play like a child in the sand. It was their honeymoon when everything should have been happiness; but there was a dark place in Ty's heart that could never come into the sunlight and laugh.

"So serious!" she mocked. "So gloomy! Smile for me, smile!"

She tossed sand on him, scooping it up with her hands.

"I was working," Ty protested. "I was thinking."

"But such serious thoughts! Why must you write such bad things, Ty? Why such ugly things?"

And then he had laughed.

"You sound like one of my critics," he said.

"But you write such angry plays. Are you really so angry?"

It was impossible not to love her when she looked at him in that way. He tried to explain to her that he wasn't angry—that it was the world that was angry. The world was hard and cruel, full of hunger and killing.

"Not everyone lives as we live, Julie."

And then the words caught in his throat as he remembered where he had found her and from whence she had come. Her child-like eyes were staring at him in wonder—eyes that had seen and lived through more horrors than he would ever know. Julie, with her bare toes digging into the sand, listening to him as if he were the teacher of life and she had never lived.

"But," she said, "there is no place without beauty. Nothing is really so terrible!"

Call her a woman and say that she would never understand. Call her a child and say that she would never grow up. Call her lovely and take her in your arms. . . .

But it was only a flame-colored cushion. Ty crushed it in his hands and hurled it across the room. The beach was gone, the sun was gone, the sound of laughter was gone. There was only the gray sky above and the relentless rain. He continued the search. Now he was hurried and careless.

He did foolish things. He tore open cupboards and pulled out drawers. He looked in places where no typewriter could ever be. He found a stack of old newspapers and a photograph.

Dana Quist was a collector of strange items. Ty examined the newspapers carefully—November 3rd, the day the story of Mary Brownlee's murder broke. Another from November 9th, when the case burst over the front page again when Mike Flanders was picked up in Las Vegas. Yes, Lieutenant Janus was right; his picture had been in the newspaper. In addition, there were several editions featuring stories on the Malibu Canyon fire in the first week of December; but it was the first front page and the photograph that held Ty's interest so completely that he barely caught the sound of a motor pulling into the garage.

Ty dropped the newspaper on the work table. He looked about him—there was another exit in the studio. He crossed quickly and tried the door. How like Dana to lock one door and leave the other open. There was no time to fumble with the catch. The car had braked to a crunching halt amid the assorted debris, and Dana, slamming the door behind him, strode into the room. Ty leaned back against the wall. His hand touched, teetered and steadied a heavy glass vase on the radio. It was still in his hand when Dana began to turn. There was an almost magnetic contact between the vase and Dana's head.

Dana went down. Ty knelt beside him long enough to make sure he was only stunned, and then fled. He had what he'd come after in a small glass jar in his pocket. He had somewhat more in the memory of a pile of old newspapers.

"It's Dana," Marcus said. "Look, Alex, he's bleeding!"

Alex hardly heard the words. She ran toward him.

"Dana—Dana. What happened? Are you hurt?"

For a little while there was nothing but Alex being a distraught woman, with no time for any real explanation until she could get Dana back inside, wash his wound with Marcus' doubtful assistance, and get him stretched out on one of the couches. Even when he could talk, there was nothing Dana could say.

"I didn't see who it was. There was only time for a glimpse—"

"Was it a man?" Alex asked. "Perhaps he's still on the premises. Perhaps he's stolen something. Marcus—"

Alex was pale, her sharp features seeming to draw tighter under tension. She turned toward Marcus. He was standing motionless before the sink. She left Dana on the couch and came to him.

"What is it?" she asked.

Marcus pointed at the glass container in the sink. The label was clearly visible.

"Acid?" Alex said hollowly. "Dana, someone has been at your nitric acid—"

And then her voice failed. There was fear in her eyes when she looked at Marcus again.

"Ty—"

Her lips formed the name, and Marcus' eyes understood. But why? she was pleading. What did Ty want with nitric acid? It was an unspoken question neither of them could answer and both of them temporarily forgot as soon as they discovered what Ty had left on the work table just beyond the sink. Old newspapers and a photograph: two likenesses of two women placed side by side so that, together, no one could fail to make the obvious association.

Mary Brownlee's photo had a newsprint blur and unprofessional plainness; Julie's was glossy and glamorous. But the likenesses were so striking that the two women might have been sisters.

Chapter Seven

Cole Riley had aged since morning. It was more than just weariness; it was worry. He poured himself a generous Scotch and soda from the small wall bar in the living room of his bachelor apartment, and then turned to face his guests. Alex sat stiffly on the edge of a black sofa, her face taut and her right hand clutching an untouched drink in a squat glass. Marcus, apparently absorbed with a framed map of 19th-century Paris, stood nearby, his own drink almost finished. Cole drank deeply and then said—

"But Dana wasn't badly hurt, was he?"

"Dana is bearing up bravely," Marcus murmured, not taking his eyes from the map. "He's of rugged stock. Alex bathed his wound and tucked him in with a strong sedative. He may snap out of this with only two or three visits to his analyst."

"Marcus," Alex protested, "this is serious!"

"Yes, I am willing to agree that it is," Cole acknowledged. "This whole thing is getting out of hand. I don't know if Ty's serious about convicting himself of Flanders' crime, or if he's simply unbalanced by grief. We know his emotional make-up."

"Conveniently," Marcus said.

Cole had lowered his head to take another deep draught from his glass. At Marcus' words, he glanced up. Marcus was still absorbed in the map, and before Cole could question him farther, Alex spoke.

"He's sick," she insisted. "That's what I tried to tell you this morning. Maybe now you'll believe me. He must intend to go ahead with his plan. I know it's not rational; but what other reason would he have had for taking that acid from Dana's studio?"

"You're not certain that it was Ty," Cole protested. "Dana didn't see him."

"But who else could it have been? Who else would be interested in the Flanders case and also know the studio was there. It can't be seen from the oceanside, and from the street it's only another garage. Be reasonable, Cole. It had to be one of us. It wasn't Marcus—he was with me. It wasn't Dana—he was struck down."

Cole smiled grimly over the rim of his glass.

"That leaves me," he said.

"Don't be ridiculous! Why would you do such a thing? Besides, you were in court."

"Yes," Cole said bitterly. "I was in court."

It was quite dark now, and the rain had settled down to spend the night. Cole stepped across the room and pulled the drapery cord, and a soft white fabric slid across the windows to hold out the darkness and the rain. He turned slowly.

"Acid," he mused.

"Mary Brownlee's face," Alex reminded. "If Ty's going to

take Flanders' place, he must have evidence of what was used to disfigure her face."

"He needs more than that," Cole said. "He needs a motive. Did Ty say anything to you, either of you, about some anonymous letters Julie had received?"

"Letters?"

Alex spoke the word. Marcus turned away from the map, frowning.

"Not to me," he said. "Were there letters?"

Cole drained his glass and put it back on the bar. Out of one coat pocket he withdrew the folded sheet of paper taken from the typewriter in his office. A fragment of one letter was on it. He handed it to Alex, and Marcus moved over to the sofa to share her curiosity.

After reading, both looked up—puzzled.

"Ty quoted these lines to me last night," Cole explained. "Today he tapped them out on the typewriter in my office. Supposedly, they're the reason behind that wild suicide stunt last night. He accuses society of having broken up his marriage."

"Oh, no," Marcus protested.

"That's what he told me last night. 'The Mrs. Herberts of the world,' he said. Mrs. Herbert is Washburn's prize witness. She'll go onto the stand and testify that she heard Flanders quarreling with Mary the night before her death—that he threatened her with violence and then slammed out of her room leaving Mary sobbing hysterically. Mrs. Herbert will swear that it was Flanders because she saw him through the window. Mrs. Herbert is the neighborhood spy. No rooming-house area is complete without one."

"Then Ty's scheme wouldn't have a chance," Alex said. She smiled nervously. "Why are we so upset?"

"Because all of what I've just told you occurred the night before the murder," Cole reminded. "Nobody actually saw Flanders on the premises on the night when Mary was killed. Nobody—"

The word lingered in the air for further meditation. What it meant was that the field was wide open for an alternative murderer—any murderer at all.

"But this—this is nonsense," Marcus said, tapping the letter in Alex's hand. "This is ridiculous!"

"Is it?" Cole asked. "I've known Ty for nearly six years. He's never impressed me as a candidate for sainthood."

"But Julie wasn't a child!"

And then Marcus fell silent over his own words, because Julie was a child and each of them knew that. She was both a woman and a child. She loved like a woman; she trusted like a child. Alex held a copy of a poisonous note in her hand. Alex, or any other woman, would have thrown such a note in the waste basket—taken it to her husband at the very least. But Julie—

Cole knew what Marcus was thinking.

"Apparently there was a series of these," he explained, "and Julie was enough concerned about them to keep them. Ty says that he found them in her room after the fire."

"A series," Marcus repeated. "That does make it seem malicious."

"Oh, it's malicious," Alex agreed, "but it's not our immediate problem, is it? What we must do is try to anticipate Ty. Assume the worst. Assume he's really sick of life and wants to die in Flanders' place. No, Marcus, don't try to stop me. I know Ty. He's capable of anything now that Julie's gone. What was her great power, anyway?"

Marcus had said something similar in Cole's office; but Alex was exasperated. Alex liked straight lines, no obstructions, neat, mathematical answers. Cole could answer with only one word.

"Love," he said.

Alex's hand closed over the note, crumpling it into a tight ball.

"But we can't let him destroy himself! What can we do?"

"Anticipate," Marcus said. "It's your word, Alex. I think it's a good one. We must anticipate Ty. How do we begin? Why not at the beginning?"

"Last night?" Cole queried.

"No, the beginning. Think of what he's done so far. He has a plan, can't you see? He rented Mary Brownlee's room. That wasn't a coincidence."

"Of course not," Cole agreed. "I realized that last night."

"He took the room for what you termed a completely phony suicide attempt," Marcus continued. "He telephoned you, and then insured his act being intercepted by leaving the shade up to tantalize the known snooper next door. Why?" Marcus paused. No one attempted to answer, which left him the desired privilege—to give his own answer. "Ty is a showman," he added. "He was sending out advance publicity. You heard him when he saw the front page this morning—'good notices' he said."

"And he deliberately allowed himself to be seen in court this morning," Cole added. "It's for some purpose, that's certain. But to convict himself of another man's crime . . ."

Distaste and disbelief—both were in Cole's tone.

"Is it possible?" Marcus asked.

"Possible?" Cole faced him with tired eyes. "Of course not! No innocent man has ever been convicted! No miscarriage of justice has ever occurred! Why do you think I'm defending Flanders?"

The question was thrown out in anger. It isolated itself from all the other words and stood alone where it shouldn't have been. Even Cole seemed surprised.

"I'm sorry," he said. "I don't mean to shout at people. I've had a rough day."

He drained his drink and turned back to the wall bar for a refill. Marcus spoke to the back of his neck.

"Are you saying that Flanders isn't guilty?"

"No. I didn't mean that," Cole said.

"What did you mean?"

"That he might not be guilty."

"Do you have any reason for thinking that?"

Cole swung about, fresh drink in hand.

"Damn it, Marcus, I'm not on the witness stand. I'm defending Flanders, or trying to. I wouldn't be defending him if I didn't think he *might* be innocent. All the evidence is against him; but it's all circumstantial evidence. I don't like seeing a man's life taken from him on circumstantial evidence."

"Marcus," Alex said, "leave Cole alone. Can't you see that he's tired?"

"But I'm only trying to help," Marcus insisted. "Anticipate Ty—yes. He's set himself a stage and appropriated a chemical with which he could have disfigured Mary Brownlee. What next? What else must he do to convict himself of Flanders' crime? Has he established a motive?"

"The letters," Cole reminded. "He intimated last night that they were to prove he'd been keeping company with Mary Brownlee."

"The other woman," Marcus reflected. "Good. An excellent motive. And Mary Brownlee would have written the letters, of course."

"Mary?" Alex echoed. "Why?"

"In order to break up a marriage that hindered her mating with Ty, naturally. Alex, let me see that again."

Marcus took the note from Alex's hand. He straightened out the wrinkles and studied the contents.

"This was written from memory," he observed. "Have you ever noticed Ty's remarkable memory?"

"Remarkable?" Cole asked. "In what way?"

"He can recite a play, an entire play, scene by scene—if it's a play he has written."

"You think Ty wrote the notes," Alex said.

"It's logical, isn't it? The notes give him a basis for a motive. Married man becomes involved with another woman; woman becomes serious and tries to break up marriage; married man prefers wife. The motive is sound. What else must Ty do, Cole? What circumstantial evidence needs to be explained?"

Cole had gotten over his show of temper. Marcus' argument was interesting. He'd followed it carefully and was ready for the question.

"Mary Brownlee closed out her bank account on the day of her death," Cole answered. "Flanders had over three hundred dollars in his possession when he was arrested in Las Vegas, and no way to prove where it came from."

"That's right—the poker game," Marcus recalled. "How much was Mary Brownlee's account?"

"Over five hundred dollars. Five hundred sixty-eight dollars and thirty-two cents, to be exact."

"So much? Judging from the testimony I heard this morning, she didn't seem so thrifty—or so well-paid." Marcus toyed with his glass. The liquor was long gone, the ice nothing but tiny pellets that tinkled against the side of the glass. "Of course," he added wryly, "considering her physical charms and Flanders' jealousy, it's quite possible that she had income from other sources."

"That's my case," Cole admitted, "but wherever Mary got her bankroll, you can be sure Washburn is going to impress the jury with the strange coincidence of that withdrawal and the money Flanders took with him to Las Vegas."

"Then Ty must account for both actions. Flanders' alibi is a poker game. You've checked his story, of course."

"There's nothing to check," Cole said testily. "Flanders lived in a cheap hotel on Alvarado Street. Nobody there really knew him or his friends. People don't ask questions or give answers in such places. I've tried to find someone to verify that poker game, but I walk right into a wall of silence. I intend to keep Flanders off the stand. His story is too weak; Washburn will crucify him."

"Then it isn't possible to prove there was a poker game," Marcus said.

"It doesn't seem to be," Cole admitted.

"Then it's equally impossible to prove there wasn't a poker game."

The room suddenly became very quiet. It was as if they were awed into silence by the possibility of what had unfolded before them.

"Ty has a chance of success," Marcus observed quietly.

It was too much for Alex.

"But that's impossible. Even if Ty is sick enough to try to go through with his plan, no one will believe he would have had anything to do with a woman like Mary Brownlee!"

"A woman like Mary Brownlee," Marcus said quietly, "is just who he would have 'had to do with.' You saw Julie's photograph laid alongside the one of Mary Brownlee in that newspaper in Dana's studio. Dana must have thought of it." Marcus came to his feet. He was tired of playing with an empty glass. He crossed to the bar and set the glass down on the bar top. He turned around. "It's a known psychological fact," he added, "that errant husbands are most attracted to women most like their wives. Don't ask me why. A lack of imagination, I suppose. Mary Brownlee could have been Julie's double—that's what Dana saw. What about you, Cole?"

"No," Cole said quickly.

"You hadn't noticed the resemblance?"

"There's no resemblance. Not really. Not when—" He paused. "Not when you think about it," he added. "Alex is right. Physical resemblance isn't enough; there would have had to be something more, something deeper. I've gone into Mary Brownlee's character thoroughly. There wasn't much of it. She was poor—an orphan. She was tough and she was hard. She was everything Julie wasn't and never could be. Ty couldn't have become involved with that sort of woman. He couldn't have killed her!"

Cole drained his glass quickly, and then looked up as if expecting an argument.

"Really, Cole," Marcus said, "that wasn't what I had in mind."

"But you said—"

"I know what I said. I don't believe that any man, not even Ty, would deliberately try to convict himself of another man's crime. But he might try to convict himself of his own—if he felt guilty enough. There are crimes society can't punish; we all know that. Ty's been punishing himself for his own sense of inadequacy ever since I've known him. He married Julie and flourished, until she began to flourish more than he; then he started punishing her."

"That's not true!" Alex protested.

"Isn't it?" Marcus smiled tightly. "Don't tell me about my own property, Alex. Ty loved Julie; but before he loved her he loved the theater. No one can love such a cruel mistress without becoming cruel himself. Believe me, I know. I've loved no other for more than thirty years."

"But Ty didn't kill anyone!"

"No. No, I don't think he did. This is really developing into an interesting situation. A few hours ago, Alex, you thought I was suggesting that Flanders had killed Julie. Now Cole thinks I inferred that Ty killed Mary Brownlee. All I'm actually trying to do is get at what the devil Ty has in mind. Where is he, anyway?"

"Who knows?" Cole said.

"Shouldn't we be finding out?"

"How? Marcus, I can't chase after Ty and defend Flanders simultaneously. I left the nursemaid duty up to you and Alex and Dana."

"All right," Marcus said. "Where's your phone? I want to

call the rooming house where you found him last night. He may have gone back there."

The phone was in the study. As soon as Marcus left the room, Alex came to her feet. Her face was almost as weary as Cole's, and both of them wore the same dark worry in their eyes. For a moment they stared at one another, then, as soon as Marcus' voice could be heard on the telephone, Cole said—

"What does Dana know, Alex?"

"Nothing," he said.

"He must know something. He kept those newspapers."

"But he was out that night. He went to a play."

"He could have come home early."

"He didn't! Don't you think I thought of that? I saw his light when he came home. It was after one."

Marcus' voice had stopped in the study. Alex started to turn away from Cole, but his hand gripped her wrist.

"I don't trust him, Alex."

Alex winced from the pain.

"Cole, you're hurting me!"

"I want you to watch Dana, Alex."

Marcus came back into the room.

"Too late," he said. "Ty was there early this afternoon; but he's gone again now. I had a time making the old gentleman understand me; but he's promised to call this number if Mr. Tyler, as he insists on calling him, returns. I think the best thing for us to do, Alex, is get back to our respective roosts. We never know when the wanderer will show up."

Marcus waited.

"Are you taking me, Alex, or shall I get a cab?"

The pain lines eased from Alex's eyes as Cole loosened the grip on her wrist. "I'm coming," she said. But there was time, as Marcus searched for his hat, to give Cole one last whispered reassurance.

"Dana doesn't know anything," she said. "He *can't* . . ."

South on Alvarado, the night raveled itself away until there were exactly three customers in the small, dark bar, and two of them were almost beyond recall. The third stood before the one bright object in the room, the juke box, feeding it dimes and watching the little black discs go around and around.

"The world is a liar,
The world is a cheat,
But all of the lies turn to sighs when we meet . . ."

The bartender glanced at the clock and then moved out from behind the counter. The two customers draped on the stools could be pointed out, like homing pigeons; but the one at the juke box might make an argument. He stepped over beside him and placed a hand on his shoulder.

"Better make this the last play, pal," he said. "I've got to keep my license."

The man stood silently, still watching the disc spin.

"She had a real fine voice," the bartender said. "Unusual, you know. Deep down."

"Heart," Ty said.

"That's what I mean—heart."

They listened to a few bars more and then—

"Halloween night," Ty said.

"Look, I told you. I don't remember. I was busy."

"A Gay Nineties costume," Ty said. "Red. Red and gold."

"Okay, maybe yes—but maybe no. I don't want to get mixed up with the law. I've got a family."

"Look, I told you," Ty said, borrowing the bartender's words, "I'm not the law. I want to find somebody who knew Mike Flanders."

"I know what you told me. I know faces. I don't know names. Now knock it off. As soon as the record ends—out!"

The record ended. Julie's voice died away and the black disc slid back into the stack. Ty didn't have to see the label to know what was on it. There was a gold replica mounted on Julie's bedroom wall. It had been the hit number from her first film—a full-color musical with a ridiculous title. They had called it "Diamond Jim Rock."

Chapter Eight

The second day of the Flanders trial drew as big a crowd of spectators as the first—Herman Gruenther, hero of the first day, was now past history; and there was a sense of expectancy in the court, as if the momentum of events was beginning to build toward the already foreseeable conclusion. Washburn continued to build his case carefully. He'd drawn first blood and wasn't going to lose the advantage. Gruenther, the medical examiner, Patrolman Anderson, who, as on the night of Ty's suicide attempt, had been the first officer to reach the scene—each had given their testimony by the time Pearl Agnew was called to the stand.

She was a tall, pale blonde—too thin and angular to be pretty. She was aware of the fact, and had done nothing by way of personality development to offset the physical liability. She had an air of surface apology, under which simmered a growing resentment of life. Her answers were terse and unembellished. Yes, she had known the deceased for nearly two years—the length of time both girls had been employed as waitresses behind the counter of the Wilshire Boulevard drug store. Would she tell the court what had occurred on the last day she had worked with Mary Brownlee—October 31st?

"Everything?" she asked.

"Everything pertinent," Washburn said.

"Pertinent?"

"Important, or unusual."

"Oh."

Pearl Agnew stared at her hands folded in her lap for several seconds, and then began in a low, unmelodious voice:

"She came in late. That wasn't really unusual. Thursday is her day off and she usually dated her boyfriend Thursday night. She came in late nearly every Friday, looking like she had a hangover—or worse."

"Worse?" Washburn repeated. "What do you mean by that?"

"You know, like she'd had a fight. She was always having a fight with her boyfriend."

"Did she tell you that?"

"How else would I know? Sure, she told me."

"And had she had a fight with her boyfriend on that last Thursday?"

Pearl Agnew hesitated. For a moment there was expression on her face, and the expression was vague surprise.

"No," she said, finally. "That's funny."

"Funny, Miss Agnew?"

"I mean, nearly every Friday she'd tell me what a fight she'd had the night before, almost like she enjoyed it. But on that last Friday, she didn't say anything about the night before. She didn't say hardly anything at all, except what a terrible headache she had. She took two Bromo tablets before she even put on her apron."

"She was ill, then."

The witness hesitated again. "I don't know," she said. "She acted more like she was scared."

It was time for Cole to protest to the leading question, and to be overruled. Washburn could continue, with Pearl Agnew's opinion underlined.

"Did anything else unusual occur, Miss Agnew?" Washburn asked.

"Yes sir. As soon as the breakfast trade slackened, Mary went into one of the phone booths and made a call. She was in there a long time—oh, five or six minutes. I know because she had to come out once and ask the cashier for an extra dime."

"Did she say to whom she made the call?"

"No, sir. She didn't say, and I didn't ask."

"Did her manner change in any way after making the call?"

"Her manner?"

"Did she complain of a headache, for instance?"

A second expression returned to the witness' face, and this time it was pleased surprise.

"Now that you mention it, she didn't," she said. "But she did keep watching the clock. At ten o'clock sharp she whipped off her cap and apron and said she was taking a break to go on an errand. It was a lousy thing to do. The coffee trade gets heavy at ten, but I couldn't stop her. She was gone seventeen minutes—that's seven minutes more than she was entitled to."

"Did she explain her long absence?"

"She wasn't even going to mention it; but I told her she'd get fired if the manager found out what she was doing."

"What did she say to that?"

Pearl Agnew's third expression was acute embarrassment. She looked about the courtroom apprehensively.

"Her exact words?" she asked.

"Please."

"All right, if that's what you want. She said that she didn't give a damn if she did lose the stinking job, because she didn't need it any more anyway."

The statement brought a stir of interest in the courtroom. Washburn let it stand unembellished. He went on to other matters. Had anything else unusual occurred? Yes. Mary Brownlee had gone home for lunch; ordinarily she ate in the store. Had she returned on time? No. She had been late again. And then Washburn went on to what he'd been building up to all this time.

"You stated that Miss Brownlee had frequent—I think you said 'fights' with her boyfriend. Why didn't she break off her relationship with so belligerent a friend?"

"Break off?" Pearl Agnew echoed. "I don't think she could."

"Because she was so much in love?"

"Oh, no. She wasn't in love. She was afraid."

"Afraid of her boyfriend?"

"Yes."

"Did you ever see this boyfriend, Miss Agnew?"

"Yes, I did. He used to come to the store sometimes and have coffee while he was waiting for Mary to get off her shift. That's him over there—Mike Flanders."

At the conclusion of these words, Washburn resumed his seat and left the witness to Cole's cross-examination. At the same time, Lieutenant Janus quit his place among the witnesses to be called and walked slowly toward the rear of the room. His eyes were practiced and careful; but they didn't find the person he sought. At the door, he turned about and paused to listen. The defense counsel was observing;

he'd caught upon the obvious: the witness was plain and unlovely; the deceased had been lovely and wanted. He was already guiding his questions into a path that was irresistible to a jealous woman. Wasn't Mary Brownlee the romantic type? Wasn't she inclined to boast of her conquests? Pearl Agnew, who seemed to have had no conquests, followed the lead with the first show of enthusiasm since taking the stand. Janus smiled ironically as he watched. Lawyers amused him; but then, after seventeen years of watching them destroy cases he'd risked his life to arrest, Janus had acquired a slightly masochistic sense of humor. Perhaps it was just nature's way of making life bearable to be able to enjoy his own frustrations; but this time he didn't expect frustration. Pearl Agnew's testimony could be negated; she was a weak witness at best. But she was only a set-up for the bank teller who would be called next. Cole Riley didn't have a chance. Flanders was guilty, and not even the brilliant Mr. Riley could build a case out of thin air.

Cole Riley. He watched a few moments longer. He was a polished performer—a handsome man in his way, although Janus preferred the D.A.'s rugged personality to Riley's social polish. But Riley was a sound man. He was too intelligent to be anything less than honest.

But why was he defending Flanders?

"Isn't it possible, Miss Agnew, that your romantic friend, who always told you of these terrible fights with her boyfriend, might have embellished the stories a bit?"

Washburn objected and Riley withdrew the question; he'd already made his point. Janus continued to listen.

"But wouldn't you say, Miss Agnew—now this is a matter of opinion, I confess, but I assure the learned prosecutor before he protests that it is pertinent to my client's case—wouldn't you say that perhaps Mary Brownlee was a little vain?"

Janus smiled appreciatively. Riley was clever. Pearl Agnew leaped at the bait.

"Oh, yes, she was that! She was more than just vain; she bragged all the time, and she lied."

"Lied?" Cole echoed. "Why do you say that?"

"Because of the stories she was always telling about her swell friends and her influential connections. She thought she looked like that singer—Julie San Martin. She made herself up to look like her, and even dyed her hair. That wasn't enough; she even said that she knew her."

"And that wasn't true?"

"Of course not! It was just talk. She was always lying."

"Then she could have lied about her fear of Mike Flanders, couldn't she?"

Riley was very clever, but now Janus' smile had faded. Now it was a frown. It hadn't been a picnic being ordered over to Vegas to take Flanders. The mean ones, the acid-throwing ones, were capable of anything when they were cornered. Flanders had submitted quietly; but he'd been drinking. Drink made some men wild and some men docile. This time he'd been lucky. But Flanders was the man he'd brought in, and Riley was the man who was trying to get him off. Lieutenant Janus frowned for two reasons. The first reason was something that had been bothering him for several weeks. That random thought again: why was Riley, who was more at home bringing consolation to heartbroken divorcees by means of $2000-a-week settlements, defending Flanders without a fee? The second reason was what caused him to turn and go out through the double doors into the hallway. He glanced at his watch. It was one minute before eleven. Keenan had promised to meet him in the hall at eleven, and Keenan was as prompt as a bank runner working for a raise. He looked up from his watch just as the elevator doors at the end of the hall opened and Keenan stepped out. Allowing ten seconds to cover the distance and he was still ahead of time. Keenan was only twenty-six. Give him the extra seventeen years Janus carried and he'd slow down.

Keenan talked as if he had to pay telegraphic rates for each word.

"See him in there this morning?" he asked.

"He's not there," Janus answered, "unless he's wearing a disguise."

"Crazy guy that. Could be."

Keenan's style was catching.

"Doubt it," Janus said.

"Then where is he?"

"Did you check the rooming house?"

"Nothing. Hasn't been there all night."

"Then one of the others may be keeping him under wraps."

"Others?"

"Riley—the Draeger woman—Marcus Anatole. Friends of the family. What did the lab report on that note?"

"Not much. The printed cancellation seems genuine. The paper and envelope is a standard dime or drug store item."

"Drug store," Janus repeated thoughtfully. "Is that all?"

"Not quite. That printing—it's not from a typewriter at all. Not any standard typewriter."

Lieutenant Janus looked hopeful.

"A European model?" he asked.

"Not even a European model—not even a Japanese. The lab thinks the message was printed with one of those kid's typewriters."

"A toy?"

"That's what the lab says—a toy. Does that help any?"

Lieutenant Janus' hopefulness turned to gravity.

"Not," he said quietly, "a damn bit."

Janus returned to the courtroom just as Cole Riley was concluding his cross-examination.

"But Miss Brownlee did mention that she was going to a costume party that night, didn't she?"

Pearl Agnew's enthusiasm had wilted into a kind of troubled timidity.

"Yes," she said. Her voice was almost a whisper.

"She did say—and I quote you exactly—'We're going to a party tonight. You should see the wild costume my friend loaned me.'"

"Yes, she did."

"And you assumed that the 'we' meant her steady escort Mike Flanders. Does it seem likely, Miss Agnew, that a woman so terrified for her life as you've made Mary Brownlee appear that last Friday you worked together, would have gone out on a date with the very person she so feared?"

Washburn was objecting before Cole could finish his question, but the idea had scored and no amount of objection could erase the concentration lines on the foreheads of the jury. Janus returned to his seat and sat down. Riley was doing a good job. The men and women of the jury were solid citizens. They didn't know the Mary Brownlees of society, the reckless, adventurous, emotional girls who lived on the fringe of sudden glory or sudden death. Mary Brownlee would have been terrified when Flanders threatened her; but she'd also think him romantic and imagine his lust was a compliment. Unfortunately, the solid citizens on juries had never felt these things, or, if they had, had acquired such a clutter of living in their minds they could no longer remember what it was to be young and poor and trying desperately for that brass ring on the merry-go-round of life. Lieutenant Janus often wondered what would happen if bad citizens were put on juries instead of good ones. The results might be worth watching.

James C. Evergreen was a good citizen. He was starting early and would go far. One day he would be manager of the branch of the California Security Bank where he was now a teller. He had that fresh, scrubbed and eager look. He probably had his receipts checked out five minutes before anyone else every evening.

Evergreen's story was pat. At exactly 10:07 on the morning of Friday, October 31st, he'd opened his window to face the first customer of the day. He was certain of the time because he'd been delayed due to the necessity of conferring with the bank manager about a dubious bill he'd found in the previous day's receipts. He had looked at the clock as he began the day's work.

He recognized Mary Brownlee because she had been banking at this particular branch as long as he had been an employee, which was slightly over a year. She always came to his window.

Evergreen smiled self-consciously.

"I always try to chat a bit with the customers and call them by name, if I can. You've no idea how the dourest customer brightens up when he hears his name. I guess we all like to be remembered."

"And was Mary Brownlee a dour customer?" Washburn asked.

"Not usually. Usually she was a real good sport; but on this particular morning, she was surprising."

"In what way, Mr. Evergreen?"

"In what she requested. I asked what I could do for her so early in the day—she usually did her banking on her lunch hour—and she said, 'Jimmy, I'm taking everything out.'"

"And that was surprising?"

"Certainly. Oh, Mary—I mean, Miss Brownlee—got her account down pretty low at times. In fact, she was overdrawn more than once; but she never closed out before. 'What are you trying to do, get me in trouble with the boss?' I asked. I was kidding of course; but Miss Brownlee wasn't."

"What was her manner, Mr. Evergreen?"

"I'd say grim, Mr. Prosecutor. Extremely grim. In view of her unusual request, I wondered if someone might be ill. I asked her and she looked at me in rather an odd fashion and said, 'Me with a family? That's a laugh. All I've got is this bank account. Now let have my money so I can clear out.'"

"And did you give her the money?"

"It took a little time to close her out. It was a checking account, and I had to make sure there were no outstanding checks. I finally gave her, in cash, exactly"—Evergreen paused to glance at a slip of paper he held cupped in his hand—"five hundred forty-two dollars and sixty-eight cents."

"And then?" Washburn asked.

"She said nothing more. She took the money and left."

Washburn appeared ready to release Evergreen for cross-examination; but there was one more question, the one all of the listeners in the courtroom had been awaiting for several minutes.

"Mr. Evergreen, you have testified that Miss Brownlee requested full payment of her account in order that—I believe I quote you correctly—she could 'clear out.'"

"Yes, sir. Those were her exact words."

"Was it your impression that she wished to 'clear out' of the bank, or to 'clear out' of the city?"

Cole Riley was on his feet immediately to protest the leading phraseology of the question. He was sustained, but the fact remained that Pearl Agnew had said the deceased no longer cared about holding her job, and Evergreen testified that she had closed out her bank account and stated that she wanted to 'clear out.'

Lieutenant Janus sat back in his chair. Things were going well. There was no logical reason for the gnawing sense of uneasiness that still dogged his mind.

There was good reason for Cole's uneasiness. He left the courtroom after a pathetic attempt to alter Evergreen's story. He had tried to force an admission that Mary Brownlee's bank deposits were irregular and reflected a source of income greater than her salary; and that her checks were numerous and repeated the reflection. Evergreen was discreet. He pointed out that individuals frequently had sources of income other than their salaries. He hadn't considered the deceased's banking habits irregular. The wedge for the 'other man' theme blunted and failed when it struck James C. Evergreen's hard logic.

In the hall, Cole met Dana, who had spent the morning among the spectators. Due to the crowds, they were unable to converse until they reached the parking lot. Even then, Dana had little to report. He had watched for Ty; but Ty hadn't appeared.

"It's a good thing he didn't," Dana said ruefully. "I owe him a lump on the head."

"Which you would love to repay," Cole observed.

"Naturally. I hate Ty anyway. I'm insanely jealous of his success."

"At least you're honest."

"Not entirely. I'm too poor to be completely honest. It's quite an expensive hobby, you know. Only the upper brackets can afford it."

There was an undercurrent of resentment in Dana's words. His humor was too sardonic to be amusing. Cole hesitated, his hand on the door of his car.

"Speaking of hobbies," he said, "I didn't know until last night that you collected old newspapers."

"Coincidence," Dana said. "I just happened to get a few copies in that drawer by mistake."

"Do you expect me to believe that?"

"Why not? You had me sit in that courtroom all day in the expectation that Ty would come back. You'll never find him that way. You'll never find him any way at all until he's ready to show himself. The reason is simple: you're color blind."

Chapter Nine

The colors were red and blue and white; it was a most patriotic juke box. Ty had, by this time, made a large mental collection of juke boxes, having watched and played them in half a dozen places where Mike Flanders might have spent his evenings. Julie was on most of them. Since her death, there had been a great demand for her records. The public was morbid but didn't know it. Sentiment and reverence were words it used for the love of death.

But the search was still fruitless. Mike Flanders? Sure, he's the guy on trial for killing Mary Brownlee. Say, it's time for the news on TV. Stop feeding that juke box and we'll see how it's going. Ty took the bartender's advice and moved to a stool in sight of the screen. There was only a brief coverage of the trial; the day hadn't been as exciting as the previous one with the landlord's unexpected testimony. But what Cole had promised, had occurred. Washburn's bank teller established the fact that Mary Brownlee had closed out her account on the day of her death. Ty's interest quickened as Washburn stressed her exact words at the time of the withdrawal.

"Well, I guess that sews it up," the bartender observed, as the channel turned to other coverage.

"What do you mean?" Ty asked.

"What does it sound like? Flanders threatened her, didn't he? The landlord and the neighborhood cop, and today the girl she worked with, all testified to that. So she's scared. She draws her money out of the bank and plans to leave town. That riles him, so—" The bartender broke off ominously. "Women!" he added, in a more disgusted tone. "If she hadn't had that fancy costume, she might have gotten away."

The man's logic was fascinating. Ty urged him to explain.

"Vanity," the bartender said. "Vanity, thy name is female. Me, now, if I knew somebody was getting ready to throw

81

acid in my face, would I waste time going to a fancy-dress ball? Would you?"

"No," Ty admitted. "I don't think I would."

"Of course not. You'd high-tail it out on the next plane. But a woman— Give her a fancy costume to show off her legs and she'll go to the ball with the devil himself."

"Give her a fancy costume—" Ty mused. He spoke softly. The bartender cocked his head.

"You say something?" he asked.

"Nothing original," Ty said. "Only playback. That's an interesting idea you have there. Mary Brownlee might be alive except for that costume."

The bartender beamed.

"Sure," he said. "That's how women are. They love to dress up. Show me a woman that doesn't like to dress up, and I'll show you a queer or a wino. But a man would have been on the first plane out."

Ty got off of the stool.

"Thanks," he said.

"What? What for?"

"Inspiration," Ty said.

The search for Mike Flanders' haunts could wait. Ty returned to where he'd parked the station wagon and drove to Wilshire; then he turned west and proceeded toward the Ambassador district. Mary Brownlee had gone to the bank at ten; she hadn't gone back to the rooming house until noon. During the noon hour, according to Herman Gruenther, someone had delivered a large box to her room. The costume? The conclusion might be false; but it was unavoidable. But she might not have returned directly to her room. Before the costume changed her mind, she might have done just what the bartender had suggested. Mary Brownlee had withdrawn more than five hundred dollars from the bank. Mike Flanders had only three hundred dollars when he was found. He might have lost some of it gambling, or he might since every possibility must be probed, have won the whole amount in a poker game as he claimed. One fact remained: Mary Brownlee had withdrawn the money for a purpose, and that purpose wasn't to give the money to Mike.

Ty drove slowly, watching for a travel agency. It was because he drove so slowly that he noticed the drug store where Mary had worked. A parking lot was adjacent. He swung the wheels and nosed in. The modern drug store contained almost everything.

But not a travel agency. With some difficulty, that fact was established by an awkward young man stacking cartons of merchandise on a display counter.

"The nearest travel agency?" he echoed. "Gee, I don't know. On my salary, I've never been any farther than Catalina. Oops. Sorry, mister—"

The carton wasn't heavy; merely unwieldy. It slipped from the boy's hands and glanced off Ty's ankle. Ty stooped and retrieved it.

"Wait a minute," the clerk added. "I'll bet you can find what you're looking for at the Ambassador. It's just a couple of blocks down the street. Sure, I know you'll find it. I've seen something like that in the lobby. Some of us go over for cocktails after work—on payday, that is."

"For cocktails," Ty echoed. ". . . *Check the bar at the Ambassador.*" Strange how all roads led in one direction. "What about the girl they're having the trial about? Did she work here?"

"Mary Brownlee? She sure did."

"Did she ever go over with you for cocktails?"

"Only once," the clerk said, "with me, that is. Mary was a little too steep for me. Nothing like a simple highball for Mary; she had to have those fancy concoctions served in chipped ice with a gardenia floating on top. You know the type. The fast and greedy kind. You know."

Ty knew. What the clerk was saying was that Mary Brownlee couldn't see him with binoculars.

"Thanks," Ty said, handing back the box in his hand. "I'll have a try at the Ambassador. What is this thing, anyway? An adding machine?"

Just a cardboard box with an illustration on the top of something with a keyboard and what appeared to be a telephone dial.

"A toy, mister," the clerk said. "A toy typewriter. Really writes, too. I can make you a deal for three ninety-five."

But Ty's mind was blocks away.

"No, thanks," he said. "Can't use it."

The Ambassador. The lobby was upstairs; the travel desk manned by an attractive young lady who listened patiently while Ty tried to explain what he wanted. Did she keep records of past bookings? Was there any way to check on a flight made on the night of October 31st? She stared at him attentively.

"By a guest of the hotel?" she asked.

"By anyone—anyone at all."

"A flight to what destination and on what line?"

"That's what makes it tough," Ty admitted. "I don't know. I only know the date and the name. If you can't help me, I'll have to check with all the airlines; but I have reason to believe the reservation was made from this desk. The name is Mary Brownlee."

"Mary Brownlee—" The woman started to turn toward her files, then hesitated. "Mary Brownlee?" she repeated. "Isn't that the name of the girl—?" And then slow recognition brightened her face. "Why," she said, "you're Ty Leander!"

Ty automatically ducked his head.

"You're the playwright whose wife died in the fire. I saw your picture in the paper yesterday. You tried to commit suicide."

"It was a mistake," Ty said.

"A mistake?"

"You know how newspapers are. Now, please, can you get that information for me?"

"I'm not sure if I still have the receipts for that far back," she said. "I'll look; but it may take a little time."

"I have time," Ty assured her. "I'll wait in the bar downstairs. Please try. It's important."

There could be an advantage in being Ty Leander, the playwright whose wife had died in the fire. An overworked woman behind a travel desk would make the extra effort to fill a puzzling request. She might do it only out of morbid curiosity, but she would do it.

Ty waited in a booth at the bar, staring at the untouched drink before him. Whenever he waited, the past came flooding in like time that had gotten out of order and insinuated itself in every unfilled space.

Julie never drank.

"I don't need a drink to feel good. I always feel good. Look at you! You drink to feel good and only get gloomier."

"You were born intoxicated," Ty said. "You never take anything seriously."

"But that's not true! I take you seriously. I worry about you."

"Worry?" Ty echoed. "Why worry? What does it matter if I work or not? I've got a rich wife."

"Ty—!"

"And I'm the most envied man in the country. Five hundred thousand male fans sleep with my wife every night . . . not to mention Cole Riley."

"Cole?"

"Haven't you noticed, Julie? Are you such a big star now that it doesn't matter if any man loves you?"

He had been cruel. Yes, he could be that. But cruel enough to have thrown acid in a lovely face? Something more than anger or mere jealousy was required for that; something deeper. Hatred, that was the key. Not just hatred for Mary Brownlee; but the deeper, deadlier hatred that sprang from some personal inadequacy that made of its victim merely an innocent bystander.

Ty laid it out coldly in his mind. He could think coldly now. Because of Mary Brownlee and Mike Flanders, his mind could function over the pain.

"If I'm ever murdered," Julie said, "you'll know who hated me."

Julie again. It wasn't a haunted room now, it was a haunted booth. Julie scratching at his mind like something locked out and prying for admittance. Ty looked up. The cocktail lounge was as dark as cocktail lounges were meant to be, and for just an instant he was startled by the guest who had slipped in unnoticed across the table. *Julie!* The thought leaped into his mind and then perished. The woman was taller than Julie, quieter, more remote. It was Alex's face that slowly took form in the shadows.

"I played a hunch," she said. "I thought I might find you here. Where have you been? Why are you doing this to all of us?"

She didn't scold; she was troubled. Ty's response was to take a deep draught from his glass.

"You didn't even call last night," she added. "We tried to reach you at the rooming house, but you weren't there."

Ty set his glass back on the table.

"I really am under surveillance, aren't I?" he reflected.

"You should be! What are you doing, Ty? Night before last you told Cole that you intended to prove yourself guilty of Mary Brownlee's murder. Yesterday morning you told all of us that it was just a drunken fantasy. But yesterday afternoon you attacked Dana in his studio and took a quantity of nitric acid—"

"Correction," Ty interrupted, "I took the acid first. I only attacked Dana when he had the bad judgment to return before I left."

"But why? I've seen you through all kinds of moods and tantrums, but this is senseless. Julie is gone, Ty. Julie is dead!"

It wasn't like Alex to become emotional, particularly not in a bar booth. Ty looked up, impressed.

"Why did you say that?" he asked.

Alex hesitated.

"I was trying to bring you to your senses—to make you stop this foolishness, whatever it is," she answered.

"But you said that Julie is dead, as if there were any doubt. We all know that, Alex. Julie died in the fire. There was nothing left of her but a charred body and two emerald ear, clips."

"Perhaps I wanted to be sure that you remembered," Alex said.

"Remembered?" Ty smiled wryly. "Twenty-four hours a day, awake or asleep."

"Then it isn't working."

"Working?" Ty echoed.

"You told Cole that your motive in following the trial was in order to forget Julie."

"Oh, that will take time, Alex. But I'm trying. That's why I took the acid. It's a corrosive—I looked it up in a chemical dictionary. It's used for making textile dyes, among other things. That's convenient. Who do I know who makes textile dyes? I asked myself. Answer: Dana. And we all know that Dana never locks his doors. Very convenient, Alex. Can I buy you a drink?"

Alex watched him. Her face was taut; her eyes attentive.

"You know I don't drink," she said.

"That's right. Incorruptible Alex," Ty said. "Or has scooping me up out of divers saloons in times past spoiled your appetite?"

"What are you doing, Ty?" Alex asked again.

"Playing Mr. X," Ty said. "Flanders claims he's innocent. Flanders claims he won the money he had on him in a poker game. It's no fun following a trial if everything is settled in advance. I like long shots. That's why I married Julie." Ty paused to take another pull at his glass. Alex's eyes never left his face. She was, he realized, a frightened woman. "Mr. X," he added, "is my long shot. I pretend that he exists. Isn't it exciting, Alex? Think. Somewhere in this city a murderer is at large. A diabolical killer who so cleverly planned Mary Brownlee's death that everyone imagines it was a crime of impulse and passion. A killer who knew of Flanders' insane jealousy and took advantage of it to cover his own crime. But he needed nitric acid. All right, now he has it. What else? The costume. That's a very important point, Alex. A bartender pointed that out to me only a few hours ago; and bartenders are very shrewd observers of human nature. Now, where did Mr. X get the costume Mary Brownlee wore to the party?"

Ty paused, holding his glass in midair. Over the rim of it he watched the surprise come to Alex's face.

"Where did Mr. X get the costume?" she echoed.

"The lure," Ty said. "That's my philosophical bartender's contribution. He claimed that Mary Brownlee would have left town if she hadn't had a fancy costume to wear to the party. Why else did she close out her bank account?"

"For Flanders, I suppose," Alex said. "He threatened her."

"And killed her when she gave him all her money? That doesn't make sense, Alex."

"I don't think Flanders is capable of making sense."

"No? Then why hasn't Cole filed an insanity plea? But that's beside the point. What Mr. X needs is a costume. There are costuming houses, of course; but that would leave a record. If the garment Mary Brownlee wore on Halloween was a rental, the owner would have reclaimed it."

"It wouldn't be released until after the trial," Alex objected.

"True; but it would have been claimed. I must remember to ask Cole about that. I wonder if he's thought to look for a label."

"Ty," Alex said quietly, "why don't you forget this and let Cole manage his own case? He thinks of everything."

"Nobody thinks of everything," Ty objected, "particularly a murderer. It's the pressure, I suppose, and the unconscious guilt. They always make mistakes; and they usually leave confessions behind them. Did you know that, Alex? I read it in a book. A criminal leaves behind some kind of confession, if only we have the eyes to see it."

"Flanders—" Alex began.

"Mr. X," Ty corrected. "It's the alternative to Flanders that interests me. Now where did he get the costume?"

Alex didn't drink; she played with matches. She'd taken the folder from the ashtray and was striking them, one by one. The brief flare brightened her face, faded, then flared again.

"You're making a great deal out of nothing, you know," she said. "The girl may have made the costume—or had it made by a friend."

"It looked awfully professional to me when I saw it in the courtroom," Ty remarked. "In fact, it looked very much like one that Julie wore in one of her films. What do they do with the old costumes, Alex? Store them in wardrobe, or release them to rental houses?"

"What difference does it make? Ty, use your head. I've been following the trial, too. Mary Brownlee thought she resembled Julie—yes, I saw the photos in Dana's studio. She did resemble her. She was undoubtedly flattered by the likeness and deliberately played it up. Now, think of how many times Julie was photographed in such a costume. Any kind of seamstress can copy a photo—that's one of the tricks of the trade. You're looking for threads that don't exist, Ty."

"Threads?" Ty echoed.

"Similarities—coincidences. It's only natural. Julie's death upset you. The last time any of us saw Julie alive was on the night Mary Brownlee died. Mary Brownlee resembled Julie and was killed in a costume similar to one Julie had once worn. Cole is defending Mike Flanders. That's the gist of the situation, Ty, and not a single actual thread in the whole picture. There's a rational explanation for all of the seeming coincidences—except, perhaps, Cole's defense of Flanders. But we all have our charities, don't we?"

Sensible. If all of the other words were taken out of the language, one would be enough for Alex—sensible. Sensible and smart. And yet, she would strike matches.

"What you're saying," Ty mused, "is that you want me to stop playing 'Mr. X' and come home and be a good boy."

"And get back to work," Alex added. "It's the only cure, Ty. There's one other thing I suppose I should have told you. It didn't seem important until Marcus mentioned that you seemed concerned over the oil change in Julie's car."

Ty smiled wryly.

"I knew Marcus would relay the message," he said.

"We drove all the way out to the village near your house and talked to the station manager before I remembered. On the morning that Julie came to my house, Ty, after the fight with you, I had an appointment to preview some new wallpapers at a wholesale house in this vicinity. Julie insisted on driving me. She was too upset to stay at home, and she didn't care to go in. She said something about servicing the car—I supposed she meant filling the tank; but now I think she must have had that oil change that's worried you so."

"I know she did," Ty said. "I found the receipt."

Alex was quiet for a moment. She put the match folder back in the tray.

"And the letters?" she asked.

"You've been consulting with Cole."

"I have. So has Marcus. This may be a game for you, Ty, but it's torture for us. You couldn't have been serious about what you told Cole in that rooming house. You couldn't!"

The declaration was more than half a question; but Ty had no chance to answer. A bellboy in a red jacket was calling his name. He answered and received the message that Miss Donahue at the travel desk had the information he'd requested.

"Travel desk?" Alex echoed.

Ty got up from the booth.

"Be a good girl and pay my check," he said. "I don't like to keep a lady waiting."

It was a way of making sure that Alex couldn't follow. He hurried up the stairs. Miss Donahue had done a good job. Her information was precise. A Mary Brown—or Brownlee, the name was indistinct—had booked passage on Southwestern Airlines to Amarillo on October 31st at 11:50 P.M.—one way.

Chapter Ten

One way. When Ty returned to the bar, Alex was gone. He sat down in the booth and ordered another drink. One to think on. Because of a bartender's hunch—or call it logic—he'd stumbled onto something of greater significance than he'd expected. Why hadn't Cole stumbled onto it? Why hadn't the police? The answer was obvious. Mary Brownlee had been murdered on Halloween night. No one would expect a murder victim to have planned an immediate flight unless the airline ticket had been found in her room. It hadn't been found—not unless the district attorney was holding it as evidence to motivate the crime. There was no way of ascertaining that; but as Ty pondered the problem he struck upon an obvious solution. If the travel desk upstairs had a record of the ticket sale, the airline must, somewhere, have a record of the flight, including a passenger list. The idea was wild. Mary Brownlee had died in her room Halloween night. Why was he searching for her?

The answer to that question was two months old. Alex had asked what he was doing, and he couldn't answer because he didn't really know. He'd been blind for two months, because Julie was the light and the light was gone. But if there were a crack of light—even illusionary light—it had to be investigated. Ty paid for his drink and asked for a telephone.

There were people who always knew how to find out things. An old friend to whom he'd loaned money and never expected to get it back—said old friend being a man named Bud Ekberg, a publicist who knew somebody everywhere. Ty fingered through the telephone directory until he found the number. The sound of music and laughter in the background, when the phone was answered, reminded him that it was the dinner hour and Bud Ekberg was a congenial chap who seldom dined alone. He had to repeat his request twice before it got through.

"But Mary Brownlee's dead," Ekberg protested. "That's the girl whose murderer is being tried."

"I know," Ty answered. "I still want to know if she made a one-way flight to Amarillo on Halloween night."

"You're drunk," Ekberg said.

"I'm sober," Ty answered, "but that makes no difference. Do you check, or do I foreclose?"

"I knew there was a catch to that loan," Ekberg mused, "and it's only four years old—but, all right. I know a guy at Southwestern. This may take quite a while. Where can I call you back?"

Ty hesitated. Not at Gruenther's rooming house—Alex or Cole might look for him there. There was another place he'd haunted last night. Flanders' hotel on Alvarado. He gave Ekberg the name and then hung up the phone. It was started. Something was working that was more than just groping in the dark. . . .

Across town, in his fashionable apartment, Cole Riley was mixing his usual evening drink. Like the previous evening, he needed it; unlike the previous evening, he was alone. The day had gone badly. The press and the spectators were getting impatient. When was the brilliant Cole Riley going to shine? When was he going to stage the miracle that would justify his identification with Flanders' all but hopeless cause? A mind had to focus for miracles. It had to narrow and sharpen and crowd out all lesser matters until the inevitable flaw, the thread of defeat, would be caught in the web of conviction Washburn was so deftly weaving.

"Of circumstantial evidence," Cole muttered aloud. "Pure circumstantial evidence."

The thread must be there. But how could he find it with Ty somewhere at large playing a game of God-knew-what—and Dana, who collected old newspapers, talking in riddles? Green ear clips. The more Cole pondered Dana's words, the more being color blind had to do with green ear clips. Ty had made a special point of them. He'd also made a special point of the letters and the fact that Julie had had the Ferrari serviced. This was what Mike Flanders' defense did with his evenings. Instead of studying the notes of the day's trial as taken by his secretary, he puzzled over bits and pieces that must somehow connect. One man could explain them if he were forced to talk. Ty's conduct was getting beyond the point of his usual erratic behavior. He had to be found.

Cole went to the telephone and dialed the rooming house. Hard-of-hearing Herman Gruenther was also hard of understanding; but he eventually reported that Mr. Tyler, as he still insisted on calling Ty, hadn't returned all last night or all day today. Ty didn't want to be found; that was obvious. Cole put down the phone and then picked it up again. This time he dialed Marcus.

"This is unforgivable," Marcus groaned into the instrument. "It's hardly dusk and you've routed me out of bed to answer ridiculous questions. No, I haven't seen Ty. I haven't seen anyone but a druggist's delivery boy who brought me some horrible capsules with which I hope to kill the cold I got chasing after Ty's trail yesterday in the miserable weather. I'll probably kill myself instead, which is exactly what I deserve for having left New York in the first place. Ty is an idiot. The way I feel now, I hope he does prove that he killed Mary Brownlee. He's insane. All playwrights are insane. And he's lazy enough to do anything to avoid work—even murder."

"Marcus," Cole interrupted, "I'm sorry if you've caught a cold; but this is a serious matter. If you must make statements like that to me, all right. Just don't make them to anyone else."

Marcus was silent for a moment.

"Then the possibility has occurred to you, too," he said.

"Too?" Cole echoed. "What do you mean?"

"It's occurred to Alex."

"Impossible!"

"She said as much yesterday evening in your apartment."

"Alex didn't mean—" Cole began to protest. And then he hold out the receiver and glared at it impatiently. "Oh, forget it!" he added. "If Ty turns up, let me know." He dropped the phone back into the cradle, hesitated a few seconds and then dialed Alex's number. He waited. He could hear the telephone ringing. He let it ring seven times and then hung up. Perhaps Alex was in the studio. He dialed again. This time he didn't count the rings. There was no answer. He replaced the telephone in the cradle again. Three calls and exactly nothing as a result; but what was it Marcus had suggested yesterday? Anticipate Ty. There was the matter of Flanders' alibi. He must be working on that. Where? The hotel on Alvarado Street was the only place Cole could think of. He searched through his pockets until he found a small address book. Yes, he still had the number. His hand was reaching for the telephone once more when the doorbell rang.

Of all of the people who might have rung Cole Riley's doorbell, the least expected was Lieutenant Janus of Homicide. They had met of course. Janus was the man who had arrested Flanders; he was due to testify to that effect as soon as Washburn put him on the stand. For that reason, it was surprising to find him at the door.

"Mr. Riley," he said, "I hope I'm not interrupting anything. I know you're busy . . ."

He was a soft-voiced man, but not servile. At Cole's invitation, he entered and removed his hat.

"You're wondering why I came," he stated.

"Yes, I am," Cole answered.

"It's about a friend of yours—Leander. What's his first name?"

"Ty," Cole answered.

Janus nodded soberly.

"That's it. My wife would have known. She's a great one for knowing the names of writers. Your friend, Ty Leander, has been causing a lot of trouble, Mr. Riley."

"He's been causing me trouble, too," Cole admitted.

"I understand he called you prior to that suicide attempt a couple of nights ago. You were on the scene when the police arrived."

"Not exactly," Cole corrected. "Officer Anderson was the first man on the scene. I arrived a few minutes later. But you're right—Leander did call me."

"Why?" Janus asked.

"Why?" Cole had never gotten around to finishing his drink. Now the ice was melted and the whisky washed out to a bitter trace. He grimaced over the taste of it and put down the glass. "Can I get you something, Lieutenant?" he suggested.

"Only answers," Janus said.

The quiet-spoken ones were always like that—polite but relentless.

"Why?" Cole repeated. "All right I'll tell you why. Ty Leander is a coward, Lieutenant. Oh, I know. He's my friend and he's a successful writer; but he's emotionally unstable. He's not afraid of life and he's not afraid of death, but he's scared to death of himself. He can't stand being alone. He needs someone around to keep telling him how great he is."

"He sounds pretty normal to me," Janus remarked.

"That's what I mean. He is normal, but at a higher register than most of us. He feels things in a very special way."

Janus watched Cole's face with grave eyes.

"You're telling me that he's doing peculiar things because of the pain of losing his wife," he said.

"Yes, that's what I'm telling you," Cole answered.

"Such peculiar things as the attempted suicide."

"The half-hearted attempted suicide," Cole said.

"And sending me this letter?"

Janus brought the envelope out of his pocket, withdrew the sheet of paper, and handed it to Cole. It was the same letter he'd shown Ty at the rooming house the previous day. Cole's eyes scanned the sheet quickly.

"Where did you get this?" he demanded.

"Through the mail," Janus said.

"From Mr. Leander?"

"That's my guess. Can you think of anyone else who might have sent it to me?"

Cole's mind sped back to Marcus' analysis just twenty-four hours earlier, as he had outlined Ty's campaign. It was pat, really pat.

"No," Cole said slowly. "No one."

"It was addressed to his wife. He must have found it among her things."

"Addressed to Julie? Then Ty didn't—"

"Didn't what, Mr. Riley?"

Cole hesitated. He was about to say, "—didn't write them," but Ty was in enough trouble without adding to it.

"When did you get this?" he asked instead.

"Little better than a week ago," Janus said. "Mr. Leander suggested that some crank might have found it in the ruins of his house."

"You talked to Mr. Leander? When?"

"Yesterday."

"And he denied sending you this?"

Janus smiled almost shyly.

"Now I know how it's going to feel to face you on the witness stand," he said. "Yes, he denied it, but I didn't believe him. He's up to something, Mr. Riley. He says he's writing over there in that rooming house; but I asked the landlord and he's seen no typewriter. This note now"—Janus reached out and took it from Cole's extended hand—"doesn't say much, but it does have the hint of a threat in it."

"Blackmail," Cole suggested.

"Possibly. It made me curious. Supposing Mr. Leander did send me the note, in spite of his denial. Suppose he has some reason for wanting to attract attention to himself in the room where Mary Brownlee died. An attempted suicide was sure a good way."

"Lieutenant," Cole protested, "that wasn't a genuine attempt. Mr. Leander was drunk."

"Just the same, it did attract attention," Janus continued. "I decided to see if there was any reason why he should be interested in that woman. Do you know what I found?"

Cole walked to the bar and set down his unfinished drink. He turned and faced Janus.

"Yes, I think I do," he said.

"You knew about it, then?"

"Lieutenant, I've been a close friend, as well as the legal adviser, to the Leanders for many years. A few years ago—"

"Two years ago," Janus said.

"Yes, I believe it was two years ago. Mrs. Leander—Julie San Martin—was informed that a young woman who bore her a striking resemblance had been arrested for trying to pass a check bearing her forged name. I accompanied Miss San Martin to the police station. Mary Brownlee was very young and seemed to be very frightened. It was her first offense. Miss San Martin had a generous nature and refused to press charges."

"Did Mr. Leander know of this?"

Cole reflected. "I don't think so. He was in New York at the time."

"But she could have told him."

"Yes, she could have."

"In fact, she very likely would have told him, wouldn't you say, Mr. Riley? I mean, I'm a married man and I know my wife would tell me if somebody tried to forge a check in her name."

"I suppose she would have," Cole admitted, "but why are you so concerned about that? Do you think Mary Brownlee wrote those letters?"

"Don't you?" Janus asked.

The question was unexpected.

"Why do you say that?" Cole asked.

"Well. I'll tell you, Mr. Riley. Right from the beginning, when you first decided to handle Mike Flanders' defense, I've been wondering why you did it. You're a big-fee man. Flanders is a public-defender case."

"I've done that sort of thing before," Cole said.

"For a certain type of person," Janus admitted. "I checked on you, Mr. Riley. You've donated your services to juveniles and twisted personalities a lesser lawyer wouldn't have understood; but there's nothing twisted about Flanders, and he's no juvenile."

"He's a human being," Cole said.

"Just barely. In my book he's guilty, Mr. Riley."

"Let's leave that to the jury," Cole said.

"In my book he's guilty," Janus repeated, "and that leaves only one reason why a man of your reputation would defend him." Janus glanced at the paper in his hands. "That reason," he added, "might be something in Mary Brownlee's past that could damage one of your friends if her investigation were in other hands."

"That's ridiculous!" Cole snapped.

Lieutenant Janus carefully folded the paper and put it back into his pocket. Now he withdrew a small, folded coupon and proceeded to unfold it.

"No more ridiculous than this," he said. "I've checked at the rooming house, but your friend, Mr. Leander, hasn't been back. Maybe you'll see him before I do. If you do, give him this."

Cole accepted the coupon, his eyes puzzled.

"What is it?" he asked.

"A receipt for a tankful of gasoline," Janus explained. "You'll notice that it's all made out and stamped with the dealer's name and location; but the customer's signature is missing. The station owner called in to see if the police could give him Mr. Leander's address—because of that mess in the newspapers a couple of days ago, I suppose. When I noticed the location, I went out to have a talk with him."

Cole glanced at the address on the coupon. "Eighth Street," he read aloud. Then he studied the number. "Why, that's near the rooming house. What's so remarkable about that? Mr. Leander has been staying there. I suppose he bought gas and drove off without signing for it. He's absent-minded at times."

"I think he did it deliberately," Janus said.

"Deliberately. Why?"

Lieutenant Janus studied Cole's face soberly.

"Did Miss San Martin drive a Ferrari?" he asked.

"Yes, she did," Cole admitted slowly.

And then Lieutenant Janus told his story. He'd gone to the station to investigate the call, and Nick, the manager, had inadvertently mentioned having serviced Julie San Martin's car.

"'That's how I got Mr. Leander for a customer,' he told me," Janus relayed. "It seems that he found the receipt for servicing among his wife's things. The address was on it, so he drove over to see why she was having the job done so far from home. Nick remembered the car. It was the first one of this kind he'd worked on. He says that Leander asked a lot of questions about his wife. How she acted. Was she alone? Nick told him that she'd come in about 11:30 in the morning, waited for the car, consulting her wrist watch all the time. Nick was alone that morning. His helper didn't come until noon. It was a quarter past twelve before he finished the job and Miss San Martin drove off. A few minutes later, Nick quit for lunch. He took his car and drove around the corner. Halfway down the block, he saw the Ferrari parked in front of a rooming house."

Janus paused. Cole's eyes had already absorbed the knowledge yet to be spoken.

"It was the rooming house where Mary Brownlee lived," Janus added.

"And the date?"

"The day she was killed," Janus said.

He waited. He seemed to be expecting some kind of explanation; but Cole's face, when he looked up, was merely bewildered.

"I don't understand," he said.

"Miss San Martin never said anything about keeping in touch with Mary Brownlee?"

"Never!"

"Then there must have been a reason."

The reason, Janus seemed to say, was tucked in his coat pocket. One thing was obvious. Ty had been over the ground carefully before he pulled his fake suicide attempt. He wasn't making up his "plot" as he went along; he had a plan. And his plan included Lieutenant Janus. That was the most disturbing thing about this new discovery. Suddenly, Cole wanted to be rid of him.

"I still don't understand about Miss San Martin," he said, "but I'll give this coupon to Mr. Leander when I see him. Maybe he knows something I don't know. If so, I'll get in touch with you."

"I hope so," Janus said.

"What do you mean?"

"Oh, I don't know. I just have a feeling that you already know more about this than I do. It's a peculiar thing about the story the manager told me. Just before Leander drove off without signing the coupon, he'd told Nick that someone would be in asking about it, and that he was to tell the whole story just as Nick had first told it to him. What's he up to, Mr. Riley? What's your friend up to?"

There was only one answer Cole could give honestly.

"I don't know," he said.

Janus left. When he was gone, Cole returned to the telephone and dialed Alex once more. There was still no answer.

He could wait no longer. When something was lost it had to be searched for.

Ty didn't know what he expected. Ekberg couldn't come up with the information he wanted like a magician pulling a rabbit out of a hat. Back at the dingy hotel on Alvarado, he waited; but the telephone didn't ring. Perhaps Ekberg had forgotten. The sounds in the background of their call had sounded gay and promising, and a reminder might be in order. He went to the desk where a sleepy clerk with wrinkled brown pockets under his eyes shooed him away from the telephone.

"There's a booth across the lobby," he announced. "No private calls from this one, mister. Use the pay phone."

"The best things in life are free," Ty muttered glumly, but he went to the booth all the same. The light was out in the booth, and he had to step outside to look up Ekberg's number in the directory. He was no good at remembering telephone numbers. He reached into his pocket for a pencil. If he could just write it down somewhere— The wall alongside the booth was a yellowed cream that hadn't been painted in too many years. Others before him had put it to the same use he was contemplating; but as Ty studied the wall, he lost interest in Bud Ekberg.

So simple. So open. So obvious, when the eye found the right spot to look. Mike Flanders had a friend with whom he'd played poker, and his friend's name was Cappy. It was scrawled there on the wall before him—complete with telephone number.

Chapter Eleven

It was a Long Beach number. A man answered.

"Tiny's Corner Bar and Grill," he said. "What's your pleasure?"

It wasn't the response Ty had expected.

"Tiny's Corner Bar?" he repeated.

"Yeah. What's the matter—wrong number?"

"Maybe not," Ty said. "Do you have anyone there called Cappy?"

"Cappy?"

The voice on the other end of the wire must belong to Tiny. It sounded as if it were coming out of a bass viol. It was silent a second, and then—

"Cappy Jorgensen?" he asked.

Ty didn't know; but it sounded right.

"Yes," he said. "Cappy Jorgensen."

"He ain't here. He ain't been in for a couple of months." It was disappointing news; but it still sounded right. A couple of months was just the right length of time for Mike Flanders' poker-playing companion to have been away.

"Do you know where he lives?" Ty asked.

"Cappy? He lives on his boat."

It sounded better. A boat out at sea wouldn't be a place to follow the plight of a friend charged with murder.

"Where is the boat?" Ty asked.

"When it's in, down at fishermen's docks. But I just told you. Cappy's been out on a charter trip for a couple of— Wait a minute—"

The voice stopped, and in the background Ty could pick up a murmur that must be coming from customers at the bar. "Is that so?" the bass viol sounded. "When? You sure? Okay. A guy on the phone wants to know." And then the voice returned to the mouthpiece. "Hey," it reported, "a customer says Cappy's boat docked early this morning. In that case, he'll probably be in before the night's over. Want him to call you?"

Waiting for calls was a tedious business, and a man just in from two months at sea might not be in a mood to remember details. Ty peeked through the door of the booth and peered at the clock above the desk. It was almost eight. He couldn't spend the whole evening waiting for two messages, neither of which might ever come.

"Never mind," he said. "Just give me your address, and I'll be down to look for him myself."

Cappy Jorgensen. Ty could think about him as he made the drive to Tiny's Bar and Grill. It was a strange feeling to be on his way through the night to meet a man he'd never seen, a friend of Mike Flanders—not the best of character references. It was the wrong thing to do, of course.

He should have called Cole—Jorgensen was his witness. But Jorgensen hadn't been found, and so Ty had left a message at the desk, in case Bud Ekberg ever got around to making that call, and then went on his way.

It was a long way. He had time to think of possibilities. A plane ticket for Mary Brownlee, a witness for Mike Flanders. Two pieces of extremely important evidence that had been literally under everyone's nose. Could Cole have found them if he'd tried? He must have known about that bank withdrawal long before the teller, Evergreen, took the stand, and his mind was surely as keen as that of a speculative bartender. But if anyone else had checked with the travel agency, the woman at the desk would have remembered and had the information handy. It was obvious that Cole hadn't investigated Mary Brownlee's plans prior to her death. There were only two possible reasons for that. As for the telephone number scrawled on the wall near a phone booth—finding that was pure chance.

It was dark and it was lonely. Once he'd left the Freeway, Ty was more aware of his loneliness. Cities went to sleep early on mid-week nights. He drove down a stretch of wide emptiness, lined with used-car lots and dark-faced stores, and only spasmodically passing oncoming headlights, or catching the gleam of incandescent eyes in the rear-view mirror. After a few miles, he pulled to the curb and searched through the glove compartment. He removed a package of adhesive bands, a stale chocolate bar, a claw hammer and, finally, a street guide. By the light of the dash he got his bearings. He looked up. Where, an instant before, there had been headlights glowing in the rear-view mirror, now there was only darkness. No one had passed him. He looked back. Halfway down the block, he could make out the dim outline of a car parked in the shadows. For just an instant he was filled with a strange apprehension; and then he smiled in the darkness. It was an almost empty street, and some people weren't lonely. He dropped the guide amid the debris on the seat and drove on.

But now he knew that he was scared, and it was a good thing to know. The senses were a man's best friends when he walked into danger, and a witness who had been missing so long could be danger, Ty's mute senses were warning.

It was just an ordinary restaurant—a row of booths on one side of the wall, and an old-fashioned bar running the full length of the other. A soiled, limp curtain of some thick brown cloth hung from a brass bar to cover the lower half of the windows, and above, lettered in chipped gold paint, the lengthy name fanned out in an arc against the pane. Just a corner bar and restaurant—one bright wedge at the end of a narrow, shabby street lined with grill-shuttered shops and steel-gated warehouses that were now dark and silent. Ty had parked the station wagon a short distance from the corner just beyond an alley that poked like a black hole into nowhere. There was a slight mist from the sea, and the smell of oil from Signal Hill clung to it and mingled with the acrid fragrances of salt, fish, and the various odors of the land mammal, man, several of whom were crouched in various positions on the stools along the bar: some solemn as monastic mystics contemplating the amber-filled glasses before them; some animated and joyful; some quarrelsome and sullen. The booths were mostly empty. It was too late for dining. It was time for the drinking to become serious.

Ty went to the bar. He recognized Tiny at once. The bass viol voice encased in about two hundred and fifty pounds of flesh. He asked for Cappy Jorgensen.

"You the fella that telephoned?" Tiny asked.

"I'm the fellow who telephoned," Ty said.

"In the back booth. Way in back. Maybe he'll talk to you—maybe not. I don't know what shape he's in by this time. It's his first night in for a long time."

Ty went to the back of the room. In the rear booth, a cubicle dimly lighted by a distant overhead fixture, he found a huge, shaggy man wearing a thick knit sweater and a soiled seaman's cap. From under the cap, tufts of long uncut hair of a light blond hue protruded unevenly and a matching growth of several weeks' duration covered the lower portion of his face. Above the growth a straight, prominent nose; above the nose eyes that were blue and alert in spite of a telltale glaze that could have come only from the whisky missing out of the bottle on the table before him. Jorgensen was alone. He didn't seem to be expecting anyone; but he made no protest when Ty, after standing unnoticed for a few seconds, slipped into the booth and faced him across the table.

Jorgensen looked up, studying Ty's face with the glazed blue eyes.

"I don't know you," he said after a moment.

"I'm Ty Leander," Ty announced.

Jorgensen stared at him. The name meant nothing.

"I'm not chartering again," he said sullenly. "Not for a long time, anyway. Maybe never. I'm sick of people. Do you know"—Jorgensen leaned forward to give emphasis to his words. Under that blond fuzz, he was a comparatively young man. He was also comparatively drunk—"what it's like to be at sea for two months—*two months*—with four crazy men? Four men who'd never been to sea before, and ain't ever going again if I can help it! Fishing! All they wanted was a chance to get away from their nagging wives and get boozed up."

Jorgensen reached for the bottle again and filled his glass. He tossed it off neat, grimacing.

"Now it's my turn," he muttered. And then he peered at Ty more carefully. "Who sent you?" he demanded.

"Mike Flanders," Ty said.

Jorgensen said nothing.

"You know Mike Flanders, don't you?" Ty asked.

"Has he got a boat?"

"He's got trouble."

"He's not exactly alone."

"In a cell at the Los Angeles County jail he's very alone," Ty said.

Jorgensen refilled his glass; but this time he merely played with it on the table top. Jail was a word that made many a man turn cagey.

"Flanders is in trouble because of a poker game," Ty added. "You play poker, don't you?"

"Depends on the stakes," Jorgensen said.

"These stakes were good. Flanders says he won nearly five hundred dollars. The state says he didn't. The state says he stole it."

"And what's that to me?" Jorgensen asked.

"Flanders says you can verify his story. He says you were in the game."

Unless he asked outright, there was no way for Ty to know whether or not Jorgensen knew the truth about the charge against Mike Flanders. He must have a radio on that boat and there had certainly been newscasts. But his face didn't betray any knowledge, and it was risky to mention murder to a man so reluctant to remember a friend.

"Mike Flanders," Ty repeated. "A big fellow. Had a girl named Mary Brownlee."

Jorgensen raised his head. It could mean that he knew of the murder, or it could mean that he knew Mary.

"Halloween night," Ty added. "October thirty-first. Flanders went to a costume party with his girl, and she walked out on him. A pretty girl. Dark hair—"

Something was stirring behind the glaze in Jorgensen's eyes.

"—good figure. A waitress. Flanders was jealous of her."

And then Jorgensen grinned, and his grin was a flash of white against the dark of his sun-and-sea burned face. One pawlike hand slapped the table so that the whisky bottle danced.

"I'll say he was jealous!" he exclaimed. "'Honey,' I said, 'you should take a sea voyage sometime. You should feel the wind in your hair, and the spray in your face, and if you get cold I've got two warm arms.' Kidding, that's all I was doing. Flanders. Yah, I remember him now. 'That's my girl,' he said, 'You keep your dirty mind to yourself!' Dirty! I just talked natural to a pretty girl. What else do you say to a pretty girl?"

"When was all this?" Ty asked.

"Oh, months ago. Months and months. I was in the city somewhere. I stopped at a drug-store fountain for a cup of coffee and this girl waited on me. How was I to know the guy on the next stool was her boyfriend waiting for her to get off duty? He wanted to fight me. I didn't think a drug store was any place to fight, so we postponed it. She got off duty and we all went someplace for a drink."

"What about the fight?" Ty asked.

"No fight. We went several places for drinks. Next morning, I woke up in Flanders' bed. By that time, we were friends. Sure, I remember Mike Flanders."

"And the poker game?"

"What?"

"The poker game."

"Oh, sure. We played poker sometimes."

"No, not sometimes. This one particular poker game."

Now Jorgensen frowned, as if forcing his mind back to the crux of the matter.

"The police," he mused. "That's bad business."

"Do you remember the poker game?"

"It's like an alibi, isn't it? If I say Flanders won the money in a poker game, he gets off."

"That's it," Ty admitted.

"What about the money? Who gets that?"

It wasn't going to be easy. Even if Cole got Jorgensen on the witness stand, he'd be difficult to manage before a jury. There was only one way to force the truth from him. Ty edged toward the aisle.

"Who else was in the poker game?" he asked. "I'll talk with some of them if you can't remember."

"No, wait a minute," Jorgensen protested. "That's all right. I'll tell you. There were six of us. It was a couple of nights before I was due to take this last charter party out—yah, Halloween. That's right. I like to have a little fun before I go out for so long a time. On the sea, I never touch this—" Jorgensen's hand reached out and tapped the bottle on the table. "Never! I'm a seaman, not a playboy. But before the trip I like a little fun. I'd asked Mike to sit in on a poker game I knew was going over in Gardena; but he had a date with his girl to go to a party. One of those dress-up things. Mike hated 'em, but she was determined. Then, oh, about ten o'clock, he called me—here. I hadn't gone to the game yet and he wanted to join me. Said he'd had a fight with his girl. I gave him the address of the place, and we met there about an hour later."

It was a story. It was the right story and the right times. 'Cappy' Jorgensen hadn't conferred with Flanders, that was obvious; but he had told the same story Mike had told to Cole.

"And then you played poker," Ty suggested.

"Sure. There were six of us altogether. I don't know the other guys. I'd just heard there was a good game going and invited Mike in. We played until the morning I had to sail."

"Two days?"

"Two nights—one day. That's nothing. I've been in games that lasted a week or more."

"And Flanders was a heavy winner?"

Jorgensen hesitated. Ty's eagerness had put him on guard again.

"He won a roll," he admitted, finally. "I never asked how much. I only know that he had a roll when he drove me down to the dock."

Ty eased back in the booth. Only then did he realize the tension he'd been under from the time he'd started looking for Mike Flanders' mysterious friend. An explanation for the bankroll—it was there. Flanders really could be cut out of the story of Mary Brownlee's death. He really could be proved innocent.

"Ten o'clock," Ty repeated quietly. "Are you sure it was about ten o'olock when he called you?"

"I said so, didn't I?"

"And eleven when he met you at the poker game?"

"That I know for sure. We had to wait an hour to cut in on the game. A couple of guys weren't leaving until twelve, and they didn't want more than six at the table."

"How did Flanders act? Was he upset?"

"Upset?" One of Jorgensen's eyebrows crawled upward as he took a slow sip from his glass. "Why should he be upset? I told you, he won a roll."

"I didn't mean that. I mean about the fight with his girl."

"Oh, that! He didn't mention it. Why should he? Who doesn't fight with his girl? How about you? Didn't you ever get burned with a dame? What's the matter, mister? You wanted to know if Mike Flanders played poker and I told you. You wanted to know if he won and I told you. What else is there to know?"

Ty didn't answer immediately. His mind was too busy with the picture of Mike Flanders and the crime he couldn't have committed if Jorgensen was telling the truth. It was more than the time element. It was the unconcern. If Flanders could have killed Mary Brownlee and then gone calmly off to play poker for thirty-six hours without even a slip of the tongue, he was more of a monster than any of the trial spectators imagined. Even if he felt no remorse, he should have felt fear. But he was afraid to question Jorgensen any more. The man thought he was clearing a friend of a theft charge; he might change his story if he knew it was murder.

"Only one thing more," he said. "Are you willing to testify that Flanders won that money?"

"In court?"

"Yes."

"I don't like courts. Courts take time, and time is money."

"A prison sentence takes time, too," Ty said, "and Flanders might not feel so friendly when he gets out if I tell him where you are."

Friendships were so interesting. Jorgensen might have been bought off and still be inclined to change his mind; but the threat carried weight. He would tell his story. He would tell it in court, if necessary; but he'd have to talk to Flanders' lawyer first.

"I'll take you to him," Ty said.

"Bring him here."

"It's a double trip that way. All the way into the city."

"I'm not going anywhere," Jorgensen said. "I'm not going anywhere for a long, long time."

He finished his drink and reached for the bottle again. It was with difficulty that he found it. One hand clutched it tightly as he carefully poured another glass full.

"Not for a long, long time," he said.

He wasn't drunk enough to be carried out and he had too much strength to be forced. There was nothing to do but leave him. Ty stood up and looked down the length of the room. There were fewer patrons now, but more studious ones. He went to the bar and caught Tiny's attention.

"When you close up," he asked, "what happens to Jorgensen?"

"He goes home," Tiny said.

"To his boat?"

"To the *Lazy Lou*—she's tied up at the dock."

"Thanks," Ty said. "I may not make it back in time."

Outside, the mist had turned to a smokelike fog and the streets were satin wet. Ty groped his way back to the station wagon and crawled in behind the steering wheel. He shoved the key into the ignition, and then let his hand drop. Slowly, the impact of Jorgensen's story came through to him. Slowly, the words ran over in his mind until they took on depth of meaning. Flanders wasn't lying. Mary Brownlee couldn't have died before ten o'clock—Cole had admitted that after Gruenther's testimony. Unless Jorgensen's story could be shaken, Flanders could not only be proved innocent—he was innocent.

But Mary Brownlee was dead. Ty poked through his pockets for a pack of cigarettes and a lighter. It gave him something to do while he tried to weave threads together. The fog would make a long drive even longer, and what would he gain by going to Cole? Cole had had his chance at locating his client's alibi and failed. Perhaps he didn't want to find him.

Because I hate Cole, Ty thought. *Because he loved Julie and I was and still am a jealous fool. That's why my mind runs this way.* But it wasn't the whole truth. The whole truth was that a man who had an important story to tell was sitting in the rear booth of a bar only half a block away; and by the time Ty returned he might have gone back to his boat and sailed off to be lost for another two months. The police. That was the logical move. Call the police. Call Lieutenant Janus and tell him the missing witness in the Flanders case was getting drunk at Tiny's Corner Bar and Grill. But Lieutenant Janus was on the other team. An arresting officer liked to see a conviction. Maybe there was a promotion for him, or maybe he was an honest cop who just wanted justice. It was still a gamble.

Ty was well into his second cigarette before he knew there was only one way to handle Jorgensen. By this time, the bottle on the table must be empty. If that wasn't enough, he could buy another. One way or another, and for reasons only now coming clear in his mind, he didn't intend to let Cappy Jorgensen out of his sight.

He stubbed out the cigarette and got out of the car again. The fog seemed to thicken by the moment, but nothing had changed at Tiny's bar. The same figures hunched over the bar, too intense in their devotions now even to notice him as he passed quickly to the rear of the room. At the last booth, he stopped. The bottle, empty, was still on the table. Jorgensen was gone.

He couldn't have gone far. The doorway to the bar was clearly visible from where he had parked the station wagon. In spite of the thickening fog, he still could have seen if anyone had come through that yellowish aperture in the darkness during the ten minutes or so he had considered his best course of action. He looked back toward the bar. Jorgensen wasn't there. In the opposite direction, behind the rear booth no longer occupied, an open doorway led to what appeared to be a stockroom. A light was burning. Ty moved toward it. Beyond the doorway, a plywood partition screened off the stockroom and framed two rest rooms. For a moment, Ty thought his search was over, and then a gust of cold air fingered the back of his neck and brought him around a stack of empty crates to investigate its source.

The service entrance stood halfway open. Perhaps Jorgensen had taken a short cut. Ty yanked open the doorway and prepared to step out—and then stopped in his tracks. Fog muffled sound even as it blocked out vision; but even the muffled sound of scuffling and blows was a sound to arrest attention. Blows—not with a fist, but with some weapon. No cries, no groans; just blows and then the sound of something falling to the pavement of the alleyway in the heavy, helpless way a body might fall.

"Jorgensen—"

He was a fool to cry out while he stood there—a perfect target in the darkness. The answer was silence, and then a clatter of metal on the pavement that drowned the sound of running footsteps until they were mere echoes in the fog. Ty rushed forward. At the end of the alleyway was the street where he'd left the station wagon, a faint blur of light at the end of a black tunnel. He wanted to see who emerged from that tunnel; but he'd taken only a couple of strides before he stumbled and fell over the heap of something in the darkness. The something was warm and sticky. The something had arms and a face barely distinguishable in the fog. The face had a beard and the stickiness was on it, too. Jorgensen. Ty dragged him back toward the lighted doorway until he could be sure. Jorgensen, with the side of his head pounded in and the life pounded out.

It took only seconds to make sure. Mike Flanders' alibi was dead.

Chapter Twelve

Everything was so very still. And sound, all movement had been swallowed up in the silence of the fog. Ty eased the body back to the pavement and came to his feet. His eyes sought the light at the end of the alley again; but he was too late. Fog. Only the smoky, restless curtain of the fog lay before him. The killer had escaped. And then, even as Ty began to follow, the silence broke under the impact of a motor throbbing alive somewhere out on the street. Ty ran forward. He was two strides from the sidewalk when a pair of headlights bored into the fog and something large and powerful lunged past the parked station wagon and disappeared in the darkness. Two red blurs of the taillights, and then the soft wall of oblivion to cut off sight and pursuit. He'd seen nothing: not a recognizable car, not a license plate, not a figure; and yet he knew with a certainty colder than the fog that he had been followed to this place, and that Cappy Jorgensen was dead because of him.

No, tell it to yourself another way. Tell the story of an old enemy, an attempted robbery, a blood-crazed juvenile. Tell yourself all the many reasons why a man who had been alive fifteen minutes ago was lying dead in the alley not a hundred feet away. Ty turned and looked back. A shaft of yellow light poked out into the fog from the open service door. The top pane of the door was a frosted wire glass. Even when the door was closed, the light would have been visible from the street. A follower who didn't want to risk discovery and recognition by passing through the barroom could have found an easier entrance; and behind the plywood partition to the rest rooms, a listener could have heard every word spoken in the rear booth. A follower. It always came back to that. A car parked a few yards behind when he'd stopped to consult a street directory. Yes, it was possible. Uncertain of his destination, he'd driven slowly; and a station wagon was easier to spot in traffic than a sedan. Ty could tell himself anything he pleased; but it always came back to the imperative that he remove himself from the premises immediately.

He opened the near door and slid across the seat, scooping the street directory, the adhesive bands, and the stale chocolate bar to the floorboards. Even then he was aware of the grim fact that he was probably the last man who had asked for Cappy Jorgensen. At least, he hadn't given his name, and the light inside was dim enough that Tiny might not be able to make an identification. Nothing could be done for the dead man; but for Ty Leander, distance was a definite need.

He drove as rapidly as the fog would allow. By the time he reached the Freeway, it had cleared somewhat. Panic was clearing, too. Questions were crowding out the fear. Jorgensen had been murdered before he could verify Flanders' story—why? There was only one answer to that. But by whom? There the answer remained mute; and without an answer, Ty was without a friend. He couldn't go to Cole now; he certainly couldn't go to Lieutenant Janus, and the story he'd driven so far to hear existed only in his own mind—and the mind of a murderer.

How does it feel to be a murderer? How does it feel to have killed a man? Ty was beginning to know the answer, because Jorgensen was dead of his own stupidity as much as of a broken head. He should have called Janus as soon as he found that telephone number scrawled on the wall. A missing witness was a police matter. He shouldn't have tried to play it alone. And then the cold knowing moved in, so that even closing the window or turning on the heater wouldn't shut it out. He had been followed—yes; but for how long? From the hotel on Alvarado Street? He couldn't go there again—not with his name on the register. The rooming house where Mary Brownlee had died? He couldn't return there now—not with a killer on his trail. And the trail was clearly marked. That had been a part of the plan right from the rope dangling from the chandelier. Now the trail had drawn response. Look for a flaw; look for a loophole; look for a way to cheat society of another orgy of revenge, and find a killer. Newton's third law was in effect. Action had aroused reaction. Curiosity had killed not a cat, but a man whose story would have given some credence to Flanders' alibi.

Some credence. Ty toyed with the thought as he drove. Some credence; but not proof. His own mind was ready to grasp at Jorgensen's story as it proved Flanders' innocence; but now he tried to imagine the mind of District Attorney Washburn and what he would have made of Jorgensen on a witness stand. He could give an alternate explanation for the money Flanders had been spending at Las Vegas—but who could say that he hadn't taken Mary's money as well? As for the ten o'clock call to Jorgensen and the eleven o'clock meeting at the poker game, wouldn't Washburn set it up as an alibi? Mary Brownlee couldn't have been murdered until after 10 o'clock when Gruenther turned off his hearing aid—but who would have known about that better than Mike Flanders? He and Mary had been lovers. How many times they must have waited until ten before going up the stairs together. Those long, semi-dark stairs. Ty's mind went back to them, and then he thought of Jorgensen's smashed head. A smashed head—a mutilated face. There was a kind of pattern there. Then he pulled his mind away from it and concentrated on Flanders again. Ten o'clock. Mary has gone home, angry and still in costume. The hearing aid goes off; Flanders returns to the rooming house. He must have had a key to the outer door. He could have gone upstairs, killed Mary, and still had time to make it to the poker game. The ten o'clock call would have been a set-up, an alibi. Yes, that's what the D.A. would make of it. Jorgensen couldn't have saved Flanders—not when the jury was so anxious to be convinced of his guilt.

And so Jorgensen had died for nothing. But that didn't make sense. There had to be a reason. Perhaps he knew more than the story he'd told. But what could he know unless Flanders had confided in him during that long poker game, in which case no outsider could have known? No, there was a quite different reason for Jorgensen's death, and this reason Ty slowly realized as he remembered what was missing from the glove compartment clutter he'd scooped to the floor. There had been a metallic sound on the pavement as Jorgensen's body had fallen. Metallic, like a hammer. Someone, apparently, was giving Ty a hand in his plan for self-conviction of the murder of Mary Brownlee.

He had been watched and followed from the beginning: Ty realized that now. It had begun with Marcus in the courtroom. *Keeping tabs on Ty.* Marcus, and who else? Alex at the Ambassador bar. Cole, the instigator of the watch. Dana? Probably. One by one he mentally scratched off the places he could go now, until there was only one place left. A place beyond even telephone service. A blackened ruin deep in Malibu Canyon. . . .

The sky was beginning to fade out behind the mountains like a spread of gray flannel wearing thin by the time Ty swung off the highway and nosed the station wagon up the curving incline that led to the house. Alex was fond of building on high places, so that the world spread out below as if it had been created solely for the visual pleasure of the residents within. She liked to use the natural terrain—the gully formed by the spring had been a particular delight, giving a moatlike separation to the patio and house below. The driveway turned in toward the high-level area where the stone section of the house now stood like a stone fortress overlooking the blackened ruins. A canyon fire was a wanton destroyer. The hills on one side of the road could be burned to stubble, and on the other nothing touched. So it was on the studio side of the gully. The grass, the shrubs, a clump of trees at the far side of the wide parking arc, were untouched by the wind-whipped fury that had left everything at the lower level in black desolation. Ty drove toward the garage—then stopped. By this time the police must have found Jorgensen's body. He hadn't the slightest notion whether or not the hammer could be traced to him; but even if it could, it would take time. Even so, it was safer to leave the station wagon in a place of easy access. He backed around behind the camouflage of trees and left the car nosed toward the highway.

Home. He let himself in through the garage doors and switched on the light. The Ferrari had gathered dust through the long weeks. It looked lonely and dejected. But it had been serviced at 11,440 miles on—according to the credit receipt Julie had dropped on the floor of the

113

car—October 31st at Nick's Service Station, 8th and Hermosa. 11,440 miles, exactly 40 miles less than the registered mileage now showing on the speedometer. That was the thing Ty had discovered the first time he returned to the house after Julie's funeral. That was the first thing. Because of it, Jorgensen was dead.

Ty walked past the Ferrari and ascended the stairs to the upper level, switching off the light behind him. The door opened into a wide hall—glass on one side overlooking what had once been a patio and a house, doors on the other leading into Julie's room and practice studio, a sitting room with a huge fireplace set in a natural rock interior wall, and, finally, Ty's study. He could never pass Julie's room without at least pausing to look in.

It was just as she'd left it. Mercifully, the fire and the firemen had spared it. There was the color of her—brilliant orange cushions tossed against a saffron couch, a pair of Abruzzi bullfighters framed above the rubbed walnut hi-fi, a gold carpet that gave like sponge rubber beneath his weight. The gold drapes were drawn and the pale dawn light had dulled all the colors with a soft shadow; but nothing could dull the memory of Julie. There was the scent of her in the room—spicy, warm, and innocent. There was the echo of her laughter and of her fury.

"I can't stand you when you're like this! I'm going in town and stay with Alex until you get over your mood!"

And his own anger answering:

"Go ahead. Go to Alex—go to Cole! Go anywhere!"

Echoes. Ty turned away and went to his own room.

He was tired. Not until he'd dropped down on the bed did he realize how tired and taut he was. A tightness had come over him, like wires strung and pulled through every nerve fiber and muscle, and his mind fought blindly against the weariness. He had to understand. He had to lay out the facts he'd uncovered and put them in proper order, because somewhere among them was the answer. Bud Ekberg. He needed Bud's report; but there was no telephone in the house. The wires had been down since the fire. But a ticket had been sold to Amarillo. Why? Why Amarillo? Mary Brownlee was a local girl—an orphan.

Run away, Mary, your life is in danger. Buy a plane ticket

and run away. Not to New York, or Chicago, or even to Miami. Run away to Amarillo, Texas. Ty eased back against the pillows and pushed his mind further. Run away, Mary; but first go to the ball. Go in a fancy costume just like the one your idol wore in her latest film. Show off your pretty body and your pretty face—make everyone see how much you resemble Julie San Martin. You'll die for it, Mary; but you don't believe that. You're beautiful and alive, and you want to be admired. Many a woman has died for no greater fault than that. Some call it exhibitionism; others call it life. . . .

Ty forced his mind until it rebelled. He slept. Exhausted, he slept on his back still wearing his coat and hat.

The pale light was brighter when he awakened. He had no idea of the time or of how long he'd slept; but he was suddenly aware of not being alone in the building.

Julie—

The thought would come, even after all these weeks. A presence in the house had to be Julie. He sat up abruptly, so abruptly that for an instant the light disappeared and his head swam in darkness. He struggled to his feet. Somewhere there had been a sound—somewhere down the hall toward Julie's room. She had come back. It was all a bad dream, and she had come back to him. He moved toward the door to the hall, only half-seeing. Somewhere between the bed and the hall one foot collided with a waste basket and sent it clattering before him. He stumbled, righted himself and went on. Julie's room. He ran toward it and threw open the door.

It was the same as it had been before—empty. A dream. Nothing but a dream. Wearily, he sagged against the door frame. Everything was as it had been since Julie's death, except that—slowly he remembered this—he was now a man afraid of being found. A frightened man slept lightly and heard sounds where no sounds were; and yet, that sudden awakening sensation had been so vivid. Could a dream be so real? Then, as he waited, another sound came. Below, in the garage, the overhead door sighed softly on its pneumatic hinges.

Ty's mind was instantly awake. No dream this: sound, distinct and clear. His thoughts raced around the studio. There was no other exit except the doorway to the patio stairs, and the patio stairs were now burned away. He could clamber down the rocks; but he would still have to pass the door to the garage level, and that door might open at any moment. It was a risk he'd had to take. He couldn't be trapped now—there was too much to do. Danger sharpened the instincts. He started toward the patio door, and then stopped, knowing that nobody was coming up the stairs.

Because the garage door had been closing, not opening.

Sharp, cold knowledge, and then Ty turned back and ran into Julie's room. He went to the windows and drew back the drapes; but he was too late. The driveway stretched out gray and empty in the morning light. The sky was overcast, but it was fully daylight now and visibility reached as far as the drop to the highway. Nothing, and then the unmistakable sound of a motor starting and an automobile driving away until the sound was lost in the distance.

No dream at all. Slowly, Ty turned away from the window. What did it mean? Someone had come to the studio for some reason and been frightened into flight when he stumbled over the waste basket—that was clear enough. But for what reason? He took a second inventory of the room. Nothing had been moved, nothing taken. He went to Julie's desk and opened the top drawer. The little stack of service-station receipts were in their right place. The crude letters, except for the one Lieutenant Janus had, were untouched. Not the desk then. He turned about, seeking the unknown, until his eyes caught on one small difference in the room. Julie had loved clothes. Her closet was an oversized walk-in, almost room size, and the door of the closet was ajar.

Even before he examined the closet, Ty knew the reason for the surreptitious caller's visit. Downstairs in the garage stood a Ferrari that had been serviced on the 31st of October. That was the first reason for Cappy Jorgensen's death. The second reason was a quarrel that had exploded in this very room on that very morning when Julie had snatched a bag from her closet and began throwing lingerie into it, and he had assisted by tossing in a blue dress and an orange. Five weeks later he'd come back to all that was left of a house and a love to find strange things for which he must pry and dig for answers. Why had Julie driven only forty miles during a period in which she normally drove four hundred? Why had she serviced the Ferrari so far from home? What did the letters in her desk mean, and who had written them? And why were the suitcase and the blue and orange dresses missing from her closet?

Ty walked into the closet and switched on the light. The bag was on the overhead shelf; and the blue dress and the orange dress hung dutifully from their respective hangers.

Chapter Thirteen

Emerald ear clips. Another marker on the trail had been acknowledged. Ty stared at the dresses for several seconds and then switched off the light and went out of the closet. He glanced at his wrist watch. He must have slept for several hours, because it was now almost eight o'clock. At such an hour there was little traffic on the canyon roads. The school bus and mail delivery wouldn't be along for some time, and the city commuters had left long ago. There was an outside chance that he might overtake the intruder somewhere along the way. He hurried out to the station wagon and drove rapidly. It was two miles to the first intersection, five more to the village. He didn't overtake or pass another vehicle for the entire route.

The tank of the station wagon was almost empty when he pulled alongside the pumps at Orin Peters' station and cut off the motor. Orin, clad in a leather windbreaker, was refilling the automatic pumps after his usual early-morning rush. He opened up at seven for the convenience of the early commuter trade and now, at a few minutes past eight, was having his first ease-off period.

"Well, Mr. Leander," he said, poking his head in at the window, "it's been a long time since you stopped by. Say, there was some folks in here yesterday asking after you."

"I know that," Ty said. "What about this morning?"

"This morning?"

"Did you see anything unusual—any strange car heading toward my place?"

Peters looked puzzled. He rubbed his longish jaw thoughtfully. He hadn't shaved and the rubbing made a slightly grating sound, reminding Ty that he must be well on his way to resembling a beatnik on the far outside.

"Mr. Leander," Peters said, "how could I possibly know if anyone headed toward your place? There's the fork—"

"Did you see any strange car?" Ty repeated impatiently.

"I've been busy, Mr. Leander. Shall I fill 'er up?"

It was hopeless. There wasn't even the guarantee, Ty realized, that the deliverer of Julie's dresses had come by way of the village. There were other roads. And then his mind caught on another possibility. He crawled out of the station wagon.

"Orin," he said, as the pump clicked off gallons, "what was it like during the fire? Was the road closed?"

"All the way to Pacific Coast Highway," Orin said. "Nobody was in here except the firemen and rescue workers. A stampede, Mr. Leander. A real stampede."

"Were all the roads closed?" Ty asked.

"Sure, I guess they were. The whole area was restricted except for the evacuees. You should have seen them, Mr. Leander. They gathered down at the ocean like people in one of those wartime newsreels. You know—refugees. And animals! Here I thought this area was civilized, but the deer and the cats came out of the hills in droves. Old man Semple, up north of your place, said the old road to Highway 101 looked like a circus parade."

Ty had climbed out of the station wagon. He stood behind the pumps, staring up at the blackened hills behind them. The fire had by-passed the village, moving swiftly across the open country and devouring everything in its way. More than thirty houses had been destroyed just like his own. The wind whipped in harder, and Ty turned up the collar of his topcoat. It was the kind of wind that had caused the holocaust, coming as it had after the long, dry summer when the whole area lay like a tinder box.

"The old road to 101," Ty repeated. "Then it was open."

Orin Peters lifted the nozzle from the trunk.

"I suppose it was, come to think of it. It's the long way out of the canyon, but animals can sense a clearing. Some of them. Some of them just panic and rush right into the fire. I tell you, it was a wild week, Mr. Leander. Well, nearly a week. It took that long to get the fire under control."

Ty listened to Orin with one ear; but his mind was elsewhere. He'd heard a motor on the road after discovering the dresses in Julie's closet; but his hearing wasn't sharp enough to distinguish which direction it had gone. He'd come to the village because that was the direct route out of the canyon. Indirect routes could be preferable for a stealthy task.

A newspaper rack stood beside the door of the station office. Ty removed a copy of the morning edition and scanned the front page.

"Got your credit card, Mr. Leander?"

Nothing on the front page. Ty handed over his card and studied the paper further—then realized it was the early edition and had been printed on the previous evening. He put the paper back in the rack and received his credit card. This time he signed the receipt before driving away, wondering if Nick had made any kind of move. . . .

Downtown, in the morgue in the basement of the Hall of Justice, Cappy Jorgensen had found a home port. But he had no privacy. It was an hour before court convened for the third day of Mike Flanders' trial, and Flanders had time to take a walk. It was a ride, actually. An elevator ride straight to the basement. For this journey, he was accompanied by one uniformed guard, one lawyer, his own, and one plainclothes detective named Janus. At the termination of the ride, he was taken into the morgue to identify Jorgensen. For the first time since his indictment, he showed emotion.

"That's Cappy!" he explained. "Hey, Mr. Riley, that's Cappy! That's the guy I told you about—the one I was with when I won that money!"

And then, by slow process of thought, he realized what that battered skull meant to him and the momentary enthusiasm vanished.

"He's dead!"

As if he should be anything else in a morgue.

"He can't tell. Mr. Riley, what happened to Cappy? Who killed him?"

Nobody made any attempt to answer. Janus had his identification. He pulled the covering up over Jorgensen's face.

"All right," he told the guard, "you can take him back upstairs. Not you, Mr. Riley. Not yet."

Cole had made no move to leave. He nodded a dismissal to Flanders and watched him go out with the guard. Then he turned to Janus. The lieutenant looked tired and a little sad. Cole's face was grave and vaguely apprehensive.

"Where did you find him?" he asked.

"Don't you know, Mr. Riley?"

"What do you mean by that?"

"Nothing," he said. "You'll have to excuse me, Mr. Riley. I got called out early before I had my morning coffee. I never make sense before coffee."

"That's not good enough," Cole said.

"What's that?"

"You had something in mind. Suppose we start over. I asked you, 'Where did you find him?'"

Janus smiled wearily.

"I didn't find him," he said. "A milkman found him on his way to make a delivery to—of all places—a saloon in Long Beach. He was in an alley just outside the service entrance."

"Was it robbery?"

"No. His wallet was on him with full identification and nearly a hundred dollars in cash. Jorgensen operated one of those for-hire fishing boats. He'd been out on a charter trip around the Mexican coast for nearly two months. He just got back in port yesterday."

"So that's why I couldn't locate him." Cole mused.

"That's why. Yesterday morning he came back to port. Last night he was killed. It looks like your man is unlucky, Mr. Riley. Convenient, wasn't it?"

This time, Janus couldn't blame his words on the lack of coffee. The cryptic allusion had to be answered.

"All right, Janus," Cole said, "what's really on your mind?"

"Where's your friend Mr. Leander?" Janus queried.

"Leander—?" Cole's apprehension deepened. "What's he got to do with this?"

"So far as I know—nothing," Cole said. "But the proprietor of the place where Jorgensen spent the night breaking his two-month-long thirst had an interesting story to tell. Last night a man telephoned the bar and asked for Cappy. That's all, just Cappy. The proprietor suggested that he must mean Cappy Jorgensen, who was a regular customer when in port. The man seemed satisfied and asked when he would be in. Knowing his boat had docked that morning, the proprietor felt safe in saying that Cappy would be in at almost any time. The man said he would be down." Janus paused, watching Cole's face for effect. "Cappy," he repeated. "That's the only name you had for Flanders' missing witness, wasn't it?"

"That's the only name Flanders knew," Cole said.

"Did you ever mention it to Mr. Leander?"

Cole reflected. The answer might be damaging if he told the truth. He decided to spar for time.

"I don't recall," he said.

"But you may have mentioned it. You are close friends."

"It's possible," Cole conceded. "What about the man who called the bartender?"

"Oh, he came to the bar—about an hour after the call. He didn't give a name, but the proprietor insists it was the same voice he'd heard on the telephone. He asked for Jorgensen and then went to the back booth where he was tucked in with a bottle. He was with him about half an hour. When he left, he asked where he could find Jorgensen if he didn't get back before the place closed. Tiny— that's the proprietor—thinks he made it back. Nobody remembers seeing Jorgensen alive after he left."

Cole had followed the story carefully. It was trouble; it had to be or Janus wouldn't be telling it. He took the side of the defense before it went further.

"Or remembers seeing the man return, I imagine," he said.

"He didn't have to return through the barroom," Janus explained. "There's a rear door to the alley—a service door. It was standing open when the proprietor closed up for the night. Jorgensen's body was lying about ten feet away; but he couldn't see it because of the dense fog."

"But you say that he did see the man."

Janus nodded. "Tall, he says, dark, unruly hair, deep-set

eyes. A young man—probably thirty-five. Expensive-looking topcoat."

Ty Leander. That's what Lieutenant Janus's eyes were saying; but Cole's said nothing at all.

"That gives you a wide field," he remarked.

"Yes, I suppose it does," Janus admitted, "but we've run into a little luck on this one. The killer left his weapon behind."

"Fingerprints?" Cole asked.

"I don't have a report on that as yet; but I'm hopeful. It was a hammer. Just an ordinary claw hammer. We found it in the alley a few feet from the body."

Cole kept his face immobilized; only his mind remained active.

"Wasn't that a bit careless of the killer?" he suggested.

"Killers are apt to be careless," Janus said, "especially non-pros. And it was foggy down there last night. If the hammer was accidentally dropped, he'd never have been able to find it again. Well, I guess that clears up the matter of identification, Mr. Riley. If you hear from your friend, Mr. Leander, don't forget to give him that gasoline receipt, will you? Nick has to get his monthly report in, and he shouldn't have to be short because Mr. Leander is so forgetful."

Another allusion. Cole stared at Janus's noncommittal face for a few seconds, and then retorted with an allusion of his own.

"I think you'd better get that coffee now, Lieutenant," he said.

Ty left the village and headed toward the ocean. It was a foggy morning; the hills loomed up on either side of the road to form a narrow corridor with no horizon. The immediate hills and an occasional house was all Ty saw on the long winding drive until a church, its spire caught in the mist, signaled the approach to the highway. Less than a month ago a small, private service had been held in that church. A service for Julie. But now the only dresses that Julie had taken with her when she left had been returned to her closet—dresses she should have returned two months ago. Ty tried to fight back his excitement, mingled with dread. His mind was full of questions that somehow had to be answered: an airline reservation in Mary Brownlee's name, a Halloween costume that had been delivered by a noon-hour caller, a dead alibi for a man on trial for his life. Get three more answers to three more questions and the puzzle that had started with an oil change sticker on the door of the Ferrari might be solved. But where to begin?

Ty reached the highway and turned south, and by that time he'd thought of another question. There had been a small, private ceremony for Julie—a closed casket and swift interment; but what of Mary Brownlee? Where was her resting place? This question suddenly loomed larger than all the others. He could go to the morgue and learn who had claimed her body; but by this time the morgue might have another entry in the death by violence lists. A newspaper morgue would be safer—and then he recalled a thing of great interest. A private collection of old newspapers in Dana Quist's studio.

Ty's foot bore down harder on the accelerator.

As usual, Dana hadn't locked the garage. Ty let himself in and proceeded toward the studio door; but before knocking he paused in front of Dana's old Ford and laid a hand on the hood. It was warm.

Ty knocked and waited. In a few moments the door opened. It was obvious that Dana had been out. He still wore a wrinkled raincoat over his dungarees. He held a newspaper in his hand; and his expression, as he recognized his caller, was more startled than surprised.

"Ty—" he said. "What—?"

He got no further. Ty stepped inside the studio and closed the door behind him.

"Early in the morning to go driving, isn't it? Or did you just get back from an all-night excursion?"

"I just got back from a trip to the Palisades drug store," Dana said.

"Drug store? Aren't you feeling well?"

"I'm feeling fine," Dana countered. "But I turned on the radio to get the news this morning and picked up an item I wanted to read about." Dana held up the newspaper. "I'll bet Flanders isn't feeling so well this morning," he added. "It looks as if his last hope just disappeared."

Ty took the paper from Dana's hand. It was the latest

edition, and the story of Cappy Jorgensen's untimely demise was on the front page. Brief, but explosive. Ty scanned the story quickly. No mention of the hammer nor of any suspect. He looked up from the newspaper and saw Dana's eyes watching him, and the interest in them reminded him of why he had come.

"This case seems to fascinate you, Dana," he said. "I never imagined you were such a dilettante of murder cases. You have some other newspapers on the subject as I recall."

He walked past Dana and went to the drawer where he'd found the old newspapers and the photograph of Julie.

"Make yourself at home—as you always do," Dana suggested.

"Thanks," Ty responded. "I just want to consult your files."

"This case seems to fascinate you, too," Dana remarked. "I had no idea you were such a dilettante of justice."

The last word was significant. Ty paused in his research duties to weigh it in his mind.

"You must refer to my announced plan to save Flanders," he mused.

"I said at the time that I hoped you succeeded. I was a minority of one."

There was no humor in Dana's words, no humor at all. Ty realized that there was never any humor in Dana. He always spoke cryptically, sometimes bitterly. The reason wasn't far behind his eyes when Ty looked at him.

"You hate, don't you?" Ty said. "You hate without the slightest provocation."

"Life is provocation," Dana said. "Besides, I don't hate indiscriminately. I only hate people."

"Even Julie?"

Dana had taken a cigarette from a ceramic holder on the coffee table. He rolled it between his fingers, his eyes grave but his mouth half-smiling.

"Ah, Julie," he said. "Julie the diabolical."

There were words for Julie, many words; but not this one.

"You must see strange things, Dana. Julie was lovely. Julie was vital. Julie was uncomplicated—"

"Uncomplicated?" Dana couldn't light the cigarette. It

had broken between his fingers. "No woman is uncomplicated, least of all your beloved Julie. She was as simple and common as an old glass slipper."

"I didn't call her simple or common," Ty reminded, "but you called her diabolical. Why?"

"Diabolical means of the devil, and the devil torments."

It was answer enough. Dana, too. Ty turned his attention back to the newspapers he'd taken from the drawer. Mary Brownlee's face, before alterations, stared up at him from the front page. Dateline: November 3rd, the day after Gruenther's gruesome discovery.

"Mary Brownlee tormented Mike Flanders," he remarked. "Is that why the case fascinates you so?"

"There's a definite physiognomical likeness," Dana said. "That may have something to do with it. I'm not sure. I haven't consulted my subconscious."

"Your subconscious be damned!" Ty whirled about and faced Dana. "I'm not in the mood for word puzzles this morning," he said. "You've got a complete file of news accounts on everything concerning the Mary Brownlee case. Here—November ninth: 'Flanders Arrested in Las Vegas'—" Ty flicked through the stack of folded papers with one hand—"November twentieth: 'Cole Riley to Defend Flanders'; November twenty-second: 'Riley Asks Sanity Test for Flanders'; November twenty-ninth: 'Flanders Ruled Sane'; December first: 'Flanders Trial Set for January fifth'; January fifth and sixth—" These were the two days of the trial. Ty's own face stared up at him from the first page of the first paper above a brief report on his suicide attempt; but the feature story was Gruenther's accusation of Flanders. The second day's edition—yesterday's—featured the bank teller's testimony; and now Dana had acquired an edition with the story of Jorgensen's slaying. "A complete file," Ty repeated. "Why, Dana? Why the great interest in Flanders' fate?"

"I could ask you the same question," Dana countered.

"You could, but I won't give you a chance," Ty said. "Don't you realize how this looks? Jorgensen is dead— Flanders' alibi. What if Flanders was telling the truth? That's what the police may start thinking."

"I wouldn't be surprised. That's what I'm already

thinking. What do you want Ty? Why have you come here so early in the morning? It's not like you to call on me. The last time you did, I got a smash on the head and you got an interesting item out of my cupboard."

"Your file," Ty reminded. "Why, Dana?"

"Coincidence."

"No. Try again."

"Curiosity."

"About what?"

Dana hesitated. He stooped down and took another cigarette from the holder, lit it, and took two quick puffs before answering.

"The obvious," he said. "Cole. Cole Riley defending Flanders. Cole isn't the public-defender type."

"All right," Ty said. "We start with Cole. What else?"

"The resemblance to Julie, perhaps."

"What else?"

Dana's face drew taut as if the skin were being pulled from behind his neck. His eyes were black with anger.

"I don't understand you," he said.

"There has to be something else. A motive. A reason. Dana, you're vulnerable. Very vulnerable. Suppose the police were to find these newspapers—and that acid you have in the cupboard. Suppose they were to hear what I've just heard you say about Julie, and then realize that you could have found a face almost like hers on a waitress at a drugstore fountain. Physiognomy—that's important to an artist. You couldn't have Julie; but you might have had Mary—"

"That's a damned lie!" Dana shouted.

"But Flanders was jealous of someone. And another thing: Mary Brownlee had met Jorgensen. Suppose she told her killer on Halloween night that she'd quarreled with Flanders and he'd gone off to play poker with Jorgensen. That gave Flanders an alibi. As long as Jorgensen stayed at sea, the killer was safe; but as soon as he docked he'd hear about the trial. He couldn't live long after that, could he?"

Dana wasn't a phlegmatic type. His fingers pinched the cigarette and dropped it to the floor. Deliberately, he extended one foot and crushed it into the deep-piled carpet. Alex's carpet. The thought registered sharply in Ty's mind.

"All right," Dana said, "I'll show you—"

He stepped to the hi-fi where a stack of records were piled; one was of Julie's songs from "Diamond Jim Rock"—her portrait was on the cover, full length and in costume. The costume was identical with the one Mary had worn on the night of her death.

"On the day the news of Mary Brownlee's death broke," he explained, "I saw the resemblance in the face and in the costume. It stuck in my mind. I called Julie—"

"You called her?" Ty demanded. "I thought no one had called her from the time of the cocktail party until the fire."

"I kept my mouth shut about it," Dana said.

"Why?"

"Because she didn't answer. I knew you two had quarreled. I could tell by her manner that night at Alex's cocktail party. I sensed the quarrel was serious."

"You sensed." Ty dangled the word between them. "Or did you know?" he demanded.

"Know?"

"The reason. Did you know about those letters?"

"Do you think I wrote those?"

"Someone did."

"I didn't! Why should I?"

"You just told me, Julie was diabolical."

Dana listened, and Dana understood. The letters were to create trouble. People who hated liked to destroy the happiness of others.

"That's ridiculous!" he protested. "I don't know a damned thing about those letters. I've tried to tell you what I do know; but if you think I'm mixed up in this—"

Dana's words stopped, as if his tongue had tripped over remembered wisdom; and then Ty noticed his eyes. This was a special kind of wisdom; this was fear. Dana was staring at the door leading into the garage. Ty turned. It was Alex.

She wore an ulster and low-heeled shoes that had made no sound in entering. Her face was severe and pale.

"Ty," she said, "what are you doing here?"

"Trying to get some answers," Ty said.

"Answers? What do you mean?"

"About old newspapers and dresses returned to closets."

"Dresses?"

Alex looked puzzled; then impatient.

"I'm glad you're here," she said. "Cole just called. He's looking for you. He sounded urgent. It's something about that sailor who was murdered last night." And then Alex seemed to pick up the leftover current of the charged dialogue between Dana and Ty. She looked at them both in turn, her last glance resting on Ty. "Ty," she said slowly, "you didn't— You weren't down there last night?"

Ty hesitated. A moment earlier he had been forcing some truth out of Dana. Now the moment was gone. It wouldn't return. But if Cole was asking for him, it meant the police were talking to Cole; and time was running out.

He shouldered past Alex and reached the door.

"Ty—no!" she protested. "Cole said to keep you here if you came by."

Then time was really running out. Ty turned briefly before he went out.

"Tell Cole I had other plans," he said.

Chapter Fourteen

Mrs. Herbert was extremely unhappy. A small, graying woman with pale blue eyes, slightly clouded by eyestrain—and she did hate to wear her glasses in public— an elongated nose, and one and one-half chins, she waited nervously in the courtroom anticipating her momentary call to the witness stand.

"Yes," she would say, when the district attorney questioned her, "I did hear arguments in Miss Brownlee's room—many times. Loud arguments, sometimes late at night so I couldn't sleep. In cool weather, I'd close my windows to shut out the sounds; but in summer I couldn't bear to have the windows closed."

Summer. Mrs. Herbert was perspiring from the strain, even though the month was January. She watched the district attorney rise to object to Cole Riley's motion. Handsome men, both of them one graying and the other still young. Wealthy men. Did either of them understand what it was to live in one room—one dingy room with just a single window overlooking an alley? Did either of them know what it was to be a lonely widow living on a pension, and prices rising all the time? An aging woman, feeling the weakness coming on and fighting it back. A frightened woman, hating the young because they were strong and because they didn't care at all what became of her.

Mary Brownlee. Dirt. *When I was a girl*, Mrs. Herbert thought, *we had a name—and a place—for such a girl. The wrong side of the tracks—that was the place. The wrong side of the tracks.* But now there were no tracks; just an alley and a window to watch because the nights were long and sleepless as the years came on.

"Yes," she would say, when she was called to the stand, "I've seen the defendant in Mary Brownlee's room. I've heard him shout and threaten her. The last time was on the night of October thirtieth—the night before the murder. I heard him say, 'You play around with me, you cross me for some high flying'"—Mrs. Herbert's mind balked. She couldn't use the same words Mike Flanders had used; not even under oath. But the district attorney had told her that she could leave them out—"'and I'll fix you so no man will ever want to look at you again!' I heard him. Yes, I'm positive. Those were his very words. And then he slammed out of the room, and I could hear Mary crying. After about ten minutes she turned off the light. I was relieved. It shines in my eyes at night when she doesn't pull the blind."

One room. Did all these fine people understand how it was to live like that? It was lonely, and it was frightening when voices shouted oaths into the night.

Cole Riley didn't shout.

"Your Honor," he said, "I'm as anxious as anyone to get on with this trial; but in view of the new evidence, I earnestly request a delay."

"There's no new evidence," Washburn protested. "A man is dead—"

"A man whose testimony might have freed my client, your Honor. I need time to make inquiries and evaluate the police findings. They may have a direct bearing on the future conduct of my client's defense."

The argument in the front of the room annoyed Mrs. Herbert. She picked nervously at the frayed seams of her black cotton gloves and waited for it to end.

129

"Yes," she would say, when Mr. Washburn pointed to the defendant, "that is the man I saw in Mary Brownlee's room. I saw him through the window many times. I couldn't help seeing him—he's so big and so loud."

And then, suddenly, everyone in the courtroom stood up. Slightly puzzled, Mrs. Herbert stood up too. To her dismay, she saw the black-robed judge leave the bench and march back through the doors from which he had so recently come; and then all of the people around her began to leave, and there was nothing she could do but leave with them. She was extremely unhappy. She had hoped to see herself on television on the evening newscast—she had even told all of the people she knew to watch for her. Now they would be disappointed, and she would be the most disappointed of all.

She was the last person to exit from the courtroom—save one. An elderly gentleman, extremely well-dressed, with his thinning gray hair combed forward over a bald spot in a manner that reminded Mrs. Herbert of pictures she had seen of some Roman emperor, waited beside the door at the rear of the room.

"Allow me," he said, executing a slight bow as he opened the door.

It was the first time anyone had made such an event of opening a door for Mrs. Herbert, almost as if it were an honor to be of service. A gentleman. A real gentleman, otherwise Mrs. Herbert would never have done what she did.

"A disappointment, wasn't it?" the gentleman remarked as they stepped into the hall together. "I'd hoped to hear some interesting testimony today, hadn't you?"

Mrs. Herbert never talked to strangers; but this man was different. With feigned modesty, she said—

"I'd hoped to give some interesting testimony today."

"You? Do you mean to tell me that you're one of the players in this exciting drama?"

It was a peculiar way of expressing it; but Mrs. Herbert acknowledged that she was, actually, Mrs. Herbert, and that she lived in a rooming house across the alley from Herman Gruenther's rooming house, with her window just opposite Mary Brownlee's window, and that what she had seen and heard in the past few months would have caused a sensation in the courtroom if Mr. Riley hadn't won his request for a recess.

"Not that I could say *everything*," she added. "Not word for word."

"I understand," the elderly gentleman observed, "and I'm sure you couldn't. It must be extremely difficult for a lady of your breeding to be exposed to such abuse."

It was as if he knew about Major Herbert, and the nice house they'd once had when the Adams district was fashionable.

"And I suppose there were other callers in addition to Flanders," he added. "Yes, I'm sure you really could cause a sensation on the witness stand, Mrs. Herbert. But, look here, why hurry off home now? I've had no breakfast to speak of. Why don't we go somewhere and have coffee and Danish . . . ?"

If she hadn't been so disappointed at the outcome of Mr. Riley's request, Mrs. Herbert wouldn't have considered going anywhere with a stranger; but he was a gentleman.

In a small hotel on Alvarado Street, gentlemen were rare. The man behind the desk wasn't at all elegant in appearance; he was, however, respectful. Respectful of the badge of Lieutenant Janus that had just been displayed to him. Janus' questions were brief.

"Ty Leander," he said, "or he may be registered as Tyler. Do you have same?"

The clerk consulted his register.

"Room two seventeen," he said. Then he glanced at the pigeon-hole boxes behind him and shook his head. "Key's here," he said. "I guess Mr. Leander must be out."

"For how long?" Janus inquired.

Now the clerk, still respectful of the badge, tried to beg off.

"I just came on duty," he said. "The key was here when I came on."

"And last night?"

"I went off at nine. Wait—Leander. Yes, I remember the man. Tall, dark, lots of hair—"

"That's the man," Janus said.

"He went out about eight-thirty. He made a phone call first."

"To whom? Did you hear?"

"I couldn't hear. He made it from that phone booth across the lobby. I make all the guests use the pay phone—always. I don't know who he called unless . . ."

The man scratched one ear thoughtfully.

"Yes?" Janus prompted.

"Well, I may be wrong, but I looked up once when he was in the booth, and I saw him step outside with the telephone book in his hand—the light's out in the booth. And then he closed the book and took a number off the wall."

"Off the wall . . . ?" Janus echoed.

"The men do that," the clerk stated. "They write numbers on the wall. I've told them hundreds of times not to do it, but they go right ahead and do it anyway."

By this time, the desk clerk was talking to himself. Lieutenant Janus turned about and strode across the room. From a distance the plastered wall looked dirty; at closer range the dirt became a haphazard design of scrawled numbers, most of them with names pre-fixed: Mable CA 1-4536; Dot, PL 7-5000; Harry's Bar—and then Janus spied what he was looking for. Cappy, followed by the Long Beach number. He had his answer. He stepped back, and collided with someone just behind him.

Janus turned quickly.

"Mr. Riley," he said. "Have you been tailing me?"

Cole's eyes were still fixed on the name Janus had just discovered. "Our minds seem to run in the same direction Lieutenant," he said. "I came in right behind you."

"No court today, Mr. Riley?"

Now Cole took time to study Janus's face. A policeman's face never gave away secrets. If he'd learned any more about Cappy Jorgensen's death, it wasn't showing.

"The judge ordered a recess in order that I might look into your findings on Jorgensen's death, Lieutenant. It may have considerable bearing on the case."

"It may," Janus agreed. "It's interesting that you knew just where to find me."

"A hunch, Lieutenant."

"Have you been here before, Mr. Riley?"

"Of course I have—as soon as I took on the case. But I never thought to look at that wall. I wish I had."

"Mr. Leander thought to look at it."

Cole smiled thinly. "I overheard the desk clerk, Lieutenant. Mr. Leander made that discovery accidentally, and it proves nothing. A killer would have erased the evidence."

"I'm not so sure," Janus said. "As I told you before, killers are sometimes careless. Where's your friend, Mr. Riley?"

"I don't know, Lieutenant."

"Then I'd better start looking for him."

Janus returned quickly to the desk.

"Did Mr. Leander leave immediately after making the call?" he demanded.

"He did that," the clerk acknowledged.

"Did he say anything about where he was going? Did he say anything at all?"

"It seems like— Yes, I got a message here somewhere."

Cole had joined Janus at the desk by the time the clerk found what he was looking for—a small slip of paper with a hand-scrawled message.

"Mr. Leander told me he was expecting an important call," he explained. "I was to take the message if it came. It never did come, at least not while I was on duty, and I don't see any other message around; but I got the name of the man who was to call him—if that does any good."

"Let me see it," Janus said. He took the paper from the clerk's hands, squinted at it and slowly spelled out a name: "E-k-b-e-r-g," he said. "Yes, I make it out to be Ekberg. Does that mean anything to you, Mr. Riley?"

"I don't think—" Cole began, and then he remembered. If he had been more alert, he would have remembered without facial expressions; but Janus' eyes never left his face, and they were eyes that read everything. "Yes," Cole admitted. "There's a Bud Ekberg—a publicist, I think. I recall meeting him at a cocktail party at the Leanders'."

"Good enough. I'll find him."

Janus moved toward the street; but it was Cole who opened the door.

"Correction," he said. "We'll find him."

On the patio beside the pool, the temperature was mild and the sun an ideal cure for a fairly large previous evening. Stretched out on a woven plastic chaise lounge, a tall, rangy man with red hair and a face that would still be boyish when the hair was gray, was talking on the telephone. His hands were busy with a bowl of unshelled peanuts that rode precariously on the tanned skin of his stomach just above the kelly green swim tights. The telephone was propped on one shoulder, hunched against his ear.

"You do think up the sweetest jobs for me," he was saying. "That information you requested is available only to company representatives and the F.B.I. You're a lucky man, Leander. That chap I know at Southwestern had to contact El Paso and the connecting line to Amarillo to get what you wanted."

Bud Ekberg was a man who rarely hurried. He paused to shell another peanut while Ty, on the other end of the wire, sweated out the wait.

"Mary Brown," he continued, in his own good time, "not Brownlee. Close enough? Yes, I thought so. Well, here's your story. Mary Brown made that flight on the thirty-first as per reservation."

After a few moments of absorbing silence, Ty's voice demanded reassurance.

"Are you sure? Are you positive?"

"Completely. But that's not all. You got me curious, lad. After all, this woman was supposedly murdered on that night, wasn't she? Isn't that what the trial's about? And not in Amarillo. So I asked my friend at Southwestern to do another check. I'm an obliging chap that way. You should be able to forget about that loan for another year for this job. All right, I'll get to it. December second. Make a mental note of that. December second. That's the date on which Mary Brown returned, via Southwestern, to International Airport . . ."

Ekberg got no further. Even from his reclining position, he could see the water in the pool, and it had now acquired reflections. Two tall, male reflections. He twisted his head, still holding the telephone in place against his ear. One of the men looked vaguely familiar; the other looked like a policeman. They were standing about ten feet away from him, waiting for the conversation to end.

On the other end of the wire, Ty was getting excited.

"Returned? Did you say returned? Bud? Where are you?"

Excited and loud. His voice carried across the patio. Lieutenant Janus stepped forward, pulling his badge from his coat pocket.

"Is that Leander on the phone?" he demanded.

Ekberg merely stared at him, one hand reaching out to steady the bowl of peanuts on his stomach.

"If it is, I want to speak to him—"

But it wasn't Janus who took the phone from Ekberg's ear. Cole said nothing. He simply stepped forward and helped himself.

"Ty," he said, "where are you? The police know that you went to Long Beach last night. They're looking for you . . ."

A loud click at the other end of the wire terminated the call. Cole slowly drew the instrument away from his ear, and faced Janus, a stoical man rapidly on his way to fury.

"What have you done?" he demanded. "He's gone. He's hung up . . ."

Which was not a debatable point. Cole smiled vaguely.

"I thought you knew, Lieutenant," he said. "Mr. Leander is a client, too."

Chapter Fifteen

Ty replaced the phone on the hook and stepped out of the booth. Cole wasn't the nervous type; his warning was serious. But the police presented only one problem: a killer was serious, too—serious enough to have killed again in order to put him in jeopardy. Because, if "Mary Brown" had flown to Amarillo on the night of the murder and returned on the 2nd of December, it could have been for only one reason. There was a headline in one of the newspapers in Dana's collection that made the reason clear. On December 1st Flanders had lost his insanity plea and been bound over for trial. "Mary Brown's" return could mean only that she knew he was innocent.

But who was "Mary Brown"? Ty walked slowly back to the station wagon, playing the question through his mind. Two witnesses for Mike Flanders, but where were they now? One was a new resident of the County Morgue; and the other— There was an answer; but Ty didn't want to accept it. A blue dress and an orange dress were now hanging in Julie's closet, and they told him the answer was wrong.

He paused at the side of the car, staring out at the ocean with unseeing eyes. Ekberg had given him another question to answer, and Cole had given him a spur. But what was Cole doing at Ekberg's house? The only possible answer was that he—and possibly the police—had been at that hotel on Alvarado Street. He was a hunted man. There was a wry twist to the thought. How carefully he'd baited Lieutenant Janus, only to have the trap sprung on himself!

Ty turned his head and looked up at the hills. Far above, he could pick out the white spot that was Alex's house; and now that sense of being watched returned. Watched, followed—to Flanders' hotel—to Long Beach. Where next? A police car drove past on the highway, and he breathed easier when it was past. Being a hunted man developed new tensions.

And a new awareness of time. Ty got into the station wagon and slipped the key into the ignition. A trip to the morgue now, with Cappy Jorgensen a newly registered guest, was like walking into a police station to ask for a street address when your picture is being displayed on a "Man Wanted" poster. But there must be some other way to learn what had become of the body in Mary Brownlee's room. Life, he reflected, was largely a matter of paper work. Birth was a legal document, duly registered, and after that a series: a diploma, a wedding license, a draft notice, a social security number, a credit rating—finally, a burial permit. Everything about a life was carefully recorded—except who it really was, or how it felt or what it thought. Or why it had died.

"Of course," Mrs. Herbert said, "I don't try to see and hear things in Mr. Gruenther's rooming house; but with the building so close, and people's voices so loud, it just isn't possible not to hear."

"How could it be?" Marcus agreed. "More coffee, Mrs. Herbert?"

The woman smiled softly. "I shouldn't really, I don't know what my doctor will say. My nerves . . ."

"Nonsense," Marcus interrupted. "A cup of coffee, a pleasant conversation—what can be better for the nerves than this? What are we living for if not a little pleasure along the way? Waiter . . ."

Such a charming gentleman. Mrs. Herbert had leaned her head against the back of the booth—leather, padded leather and soft. Not that horrible, slick, imitation material found in drug-store booths such as the place where Mary Brownlee had worked. And not a snippy little waitress such as Mary Brownlee to take the order for more coffee. A waiter, soft-spoken and polite. Mr. Anatole—the name meant nothing to Mrs. Herbert, but she did like the sound of it—had known such a nice place to go. It wasn't an ordinary coffee shop at all; it was more of a club. She began to feel quite elegant, almost as she had felt when Major Herbert was alive and they had gone to regimental reunion dinners.

The coffee came in a silver pot. Mr. Anatole filled her cup and sat back, smiling.

"And so Mary Brownlee wasn't lonely," he mused. "A vital girl, one might say."

"A wild girl, I'd say," Mrs. Herbert answered.

"But you never actually saw anyone in her room except Flanders?"

Mrs. Herbert added cream to her cup. The cream pitcher was silver, too, and the cup a graceful chinaware. Mr. Anatole was right. Such pleasures were not to be denied.

"Not *actually*," she replied.

"There were others, then?"

"Other voices, Mr. Anatole."

"Men's voices?"

Mrs. Herbert stirred her coffee with a silver spoon, smiling wistfully over old memories.

"Men's voices, Mrs. Herbert?" he persisted.

"Oh, yes," she said.

"Any particular voice that you might recognize?"

Mrs. Herbert placed the spoon in her cup and looked up, the trace of a smile still on her lips. But there was something in Mr. Anatole's eyes that caused her smile to fade, slowly.

"Any particular voice that you might recognize," he

repeated, "if you were to hear it—or if you had heard it—again?"

And then, for the first time, Mrs. Herbert was afraid.

The telephone was ringing. Two sounds: the telephone and the wind. It had risen again, blowing away the last curtain of fog until the full panorama of beach and sea stretched below the sea-gull house like the munificent offering of subjects before a throne. Alex didn't see it. In the garage, she could see nothing but the stains on the cement floor. Grease stains, marking the distance of a front and rear axle. She knelt down and applied the solvent. She waited. Upstairs, the telephone stopped ringing.

It was half an hour later when the black-and-white sedan nosed up the hill and parked before the house. Lieutenant Janus emerged and stood in the driveway waiting. The wind whipped the tails of his topcoat, and his eyes winked rapidly at the sheet of sun-silvered sea stretched out below. He waited until a second car climbed the hill and parked beside him. As Cole climbed out from behind the wheel, Janus grinned a greeting.

"You make a good tail, Mr. Riley," he said. "If you ever get tired of your practice, let me know."

"I wasn't tailing," Cole said. "As I told you this morning our minds seem to run in the same direction. You're looking for Ty Leander and Alex Draeger is his oldest friend. I told you that at Ekberg's house. Shall we go in?"

Alex hadn't answered her telephone, but that didn't mean anything. She could have been out and returned, or she might have been busy with Ty. Cole reached the doorbell first, hoping it wouldn't be Ty who answered. It was Alex. She had seen the police car from the windows, and fear was etched finely on her features.

"Is Ty—"

Cole's eyes cut short her question. She stepped back, allowing Cole and Lieutenant Janus to enter.

"Alex," Cole said, "this is Lieutenant Janus of Homicide. He's the officer who arrested Mike Flanders. Last night he came to see me . . ." Cole paused and glanced at Janus, a man capable of handling his own investigation. "It's your story, Lieutenant," he said. "I think you had better tell it."

"I wish I could," Janus said. "I'm only trying to piece it together. I understand you've known Mr. Leander for a long time, Miss Draeger."

The fine fear in Alex's eyes was well mannered. It adopted the guise of hospitable interest.

"Yes quite a long time," she said. "Do come in, Lieutenant—Cole. There's no need to stand. There's a fire in the living room. I like a fire on a chilly day. Can I get anyone a drink?"

Perhaps a bit too well mannered. The call wasn't that social. Alex realized that and fell silent.

"Miss Draeger," Janus began, "first of all, I want to ask you, have you seen Mr. Leander recently?"

Alex glanced at Cole. He could give her no asylum; she had to answer.

"This morning," she admitted. "About an hour ago."

"Here?" Janus asked.

"In the studio—up the hill, Lieutenant. The rear of the lot. A young artist, Dana Quist, lives there. I went to see Dana. Ty was there."

"But he's gone?"

"Yes. He left right after I came in."

"Did he say where he was going?"

"No. No, he didn't. But he seemed in a hurry."

"Yes, I would imagine so."

"What did Mr. Leander tell you, Miss Draeger?"

Alex hesitated. "Nothing, really. He left so soon."

"Nothing? Nothing at all? Didn't he tell you that he killed a man last night?"

"Killed?" Alex's eyes sought Cole frantically. "Cole? No—"

"No," Cole said firmly. "There's no proof."

"There may be," Janus remarked. "I haven't had a report on that hammer yet. But Mr. Leander knew where to find Jorgensen—we learned that together, Mr. Riley and me. We learned more than that. How much do you know of this, Miss Draeger?"

Behind Alex the fire was bright and warm; before Alex a policeman's eyes were hard and penetrating. She clasped her hands about her knees and tried to remember.

"Nothing," she said at last, "that Mr. Riley doesn't know, and I'm sure you've questioned him."

Janus smiled wryly. "You two stick together, don't you? Leander's lucky to have such loyal friends. But he's got a lot of explaining to do. First the hanging episode—and the letter that was mailed to me. To me, not just to the police. Then there was that peculiar business with the gas station attendant, and the story about Miss San Martin having her Ferrari serviced there. What do you make of that, Miss Draeger?"

Alex hardly dared to speak. She watched Cole's face for a cue. He shook his head.

"Ty—Mr. Leander—has been despondent over his wife's death," she said.

Janus nodded. "That's what Mr. Riley tells me. But does Mr. Leander get that upset often? You've known him longer than anyone else, according to Mr. Riley. Maybe you know if he has a history of erratic behavior."

Alex laughed. It was a forced laugh without humor.

"With Mr. Leander's temperament—nothing but erratic behavior."

"Including suicidal tendencies?"

"Definitely! That's how I met him. He was very young and struggling—oh, how he was struggling. His brand of suicide then was self-abasement and alcohol."

"And you straightened him out, I suppose."

Alex looked puzzled.

"As a matter of fact—yes. How did you know?"

"Just a guess. Tell me, Miss Draeger—" Janus's eyes were serious now. "If you knew that Ty Leander had killed Mary Brownlee—" Protest sprang into Alex's eyes, but she had no opportunity to speak. "No, let me finish before you give me an argument," Janus said quickly. "If you knew—if you were positive that he had killed Mary Brownlee and Jorgensen—would you protect him?"

It was a strange question and unexpected. Alex couldn't answer, and she didn't have the chance. The answer came from another direction—the direction of the door to the garage.

"Of course she would. Ty is Alex's satellite in orbit. She'd lie for him; she'd die for him; she'd kill for him—"

"Dana—"

Alex swung about to face him, her eyes flashing anger.

Dana smiled innocently. He was wearing his inevitable sweater and dungarees, and surveying the scene with a cool detachment that belied his words.

"Dana," Lieutenant Janus mused. "Dana Quist, the artist who lives in the studio at the rear of the lot. Thank you, Mr. Quist, for your direct answer—"

"His direct opinion," Cole inserted. "I don't know what you're trying to do, Janus. No one here is protecting Leander. We want to find him as much as you do."

"Perhaps more," Janus agreed. He turned his attention back to Dana. "You're the man Leander came to see this morning. Why, Mr. Quist?"

Mr. Quist of the direct answers. But Mr. Quist didn't answer.

"Why, Mr. Quist?"

Dana's eyes met Alex's. She had asked the same question of Ty and received no response. But Janus wasn't Alex; Janus was authority.

"He accused me of writing those letters to his wife," he said.

"Did you?"

Dana smiled crookedly. "You flatter me, Lieutenant. Leander is the writer. It's all I can do to spell my name."

"Then why did he accuse you?"

"I suppose"—Dana glanced at Cole. This was all new to Cole and he absorbed it intently—"for the same reason he might accuse Mr. Riley. Only more so. Cole really was in love with his wife."

Janus turned slowly and looked at Cole. There had been no protest to the words.

"Is this true?" he asked.

"I suppose it is," Cole admitted. "I can't see what difference it makes now."

"Did you write the letters?"

"Of course not. I don't play childish games. I loved Julie; but she loved Ty. I had no wish to destroy their happiness."

"Nobility," Dana said dryly. "Please note, Lieutenant. It's a virtue rapidly becoming extinct."

"Not nobility," Cole snapped, "common sense. I didn't think Julie deserved such a fate as Ty Leander; but she seemed happy with it. I won't say that her happiness made me happy, because it didn't! But I never heard of those letters until two days ago in Mary Brownlee's room."

Janus seemed satisfied. He turned back to Dana.

"What else did Leander say?"

"Nothing," Dana answered.

"I don't believe you. Did he say where he'd been, or where he was going?"

Dana walked to the fireplace and stood warming his hands over the blaze. He stood that way for some seconds, seeming not to hear. Then he turned about, slowly.

"He didn't say where he'd been, and I didn't ask him. He didn't say where he was going, and I didn't ask him. I didn't even ask why he came to my studio yesterday afternoon and took some of my nitric acid—or even why he bashed me over the head when I came home before he'd gone."

There was a look of swift dismay on Alex's face but she remained speechless. Janus didn't.

"Nitric acid . . ."

He turned back to Cole.

"Is this true?"

"Yes," Cole admitted.

"You didn't mention it last night. No, don't tell me. Mr. Leander is your client. Well, he's not mine—" Janus left quickly, Cole at his heels. Out on the driveway he paused long enough to remark—

"Shall we try the rooming house, Mr. Riley?"

Cole opened the door of his car.

"'Wither thou goest,'" he said.

After Cole and Lieutenant Janus had gone, Alex turned toward Dana. He was facing the fireplace again. He seemed to be waiting for the inevitable.

"Why?" Alex demanded. "Why did you have to tell that policeman about the acid?"

"Because I'm a dutiful citizen," Dana answered. He stooped and picked up a scrap of cloth from the edge of the fire. He turned slowly, holding it close to his nostrils. "I don't hide things," he added. "This"—he held up the scrap of cloth—"smells very much like kerosene. Did I ever mention, Alex, that I've been missing a can of kerosene from my cupboard for over a month?"

Chapter Sixteen

The Board of Health and Sanitation—Burial Permits. There was irony in everything, even death. It was after ten before Ty learned what he had to know, and learning it put a glaring spotlight on "Mary Brown's" trip to Texas. He left the office and found a drive-in where he could consume the breakfast he'd forgotten to eat earlier and study the situation. The stack of newspapers in Dana's studio were still clear in his mind—one in particular: Nov. 20th, "Cole Riley to Defend Flanders." A piece of the answer to the question of why Cole was defending Flanders had been missing for a long time. A fragment of that piece had been found, for on the 7th of November, the body which either was, or was presumed to be Mary Brownlee had been buried—under the auspices of its claimant: Cole Riley.

He couldn't go to Cole and ask, bluntly, why he was so interested in Mary Brownlee even before Flanders' arrest. The old reason for defending Flanders no longer applied; it had been weak to begin with. But now Cole was with the police, and the police were—where? Having no radio in the station wagon, Ty couldn't know whether or not a bulletin had been broadcast for him. He had to chance that it hadn't.

A costume that looked like Julie's. . . . The similarity was too great to be mere coincidence, particularly after what he had just learned in the records of old funerals. What was done with old costumes? He had asked that question of Alex and she had put him off. Now he would have to find out for himself. The film had been an independent production made in a rented studio. He drove across town and made inquiries. No, they didn't keep a permanent wardrobe. Costumes were supplied by the lessees. He would have to check with the particular producer involved. This meant nearly twenty minutes on a telephone before he received the required information. The costumes had been made by a supply house on Western Avenue, rented for the filming, and returned to them later. Ty took the address

143

and headed the station wagon toward Western.

The day had turned out clear. The wind was blowing strong, and the air was clean. The sun stood almost at the meridian when he parked in front of a wide-front building with Venetian blinds at the windows. The indented entrance was flanked by two open windows in which twin suits of medieval armor formed an honor guard. Inside, beyond an array of eighteenth-century courtesans, he finally arrived at a desk where a Miss Sullavan, duly identified by the displayed nameplate, listened to his story with patience and intelligence. On October 31st a certain party had called for a costume—

Miss Sullavan smiled.

"On October 31st, a great many people called for a great many costumes," she said. "That was Halloween. We do a large party trade."

"That's what I mean," Ty said. "This was for a party. A very special party. Do you remember the costume Julie San Martin wore in 'Diamond Jim Rock'?"

Miss Sullavan seemed to grow more alive. She stared at Ty, and then, quietly, she said—

"You're Ty Leander."

"Yes, Miss Sullavan."

"That make a difference, I suppose."

"A difference, Miss Sullavan?"

"I think you'd better talk to Mr. Osborne."

Without further explanation, Miss Sullavan left her desk and disappeared into the adjoining office. Moments later, she returned.

"Mr. Osborne will see you, Mr. Leander," she said. "He can answer your questions better than I can."

Miss Sullavan smiled again. Everything was so orderly, he might have been expected.

Inside Mr. Osborne's office, things were not quite so orderly. The desk, piled high with ledgers and correspondence, backed against the front windows, leaving room enough for one large swivel chair containing one slightly overweight male of late middle-age, bald, shirt-sleeved, and busily engaged in the consumption of what showed unmistakable signs of being an egg salad sandwich on whole wheat, washed down with the aromatic contents of a pint carton of black coffee. Mr. Osborne. He looked up as Ty entered, stood up, smiled, in spite of the residue of sandwich still in his mouth and extended his right hand, which already held a paper napkin.

"Sorry," he said, dropping the napkin. "Never take a lunch hour—just a snack."

"I shouldn't bother you now," Ty began.

"Nonsense! All you're disturbing now is my lunch. In ten minutes you'd be disturbing a consultation with a client. Coffee, Mr. Leander?"

"No coffee," Ty said. "Thanks."

"I might as well tell you, Mr. Leander, it's a great honor to meet you. I'm a great admirer of yours. . . . But that's not what you've come for, is it? Your wife—now there was one wonderful person. I met her when we costumed that film. One wonderful person . . . but that's not what you've come for either."

"On October thirty-first," Ty reminded.

"Right." Osborne sat down again and swung the chair about until he could reach a pile of paper folders. When he had located the desired folder, he swung back again. The sunlight from the window, coming through the open blinds, made a striped pattern on his head, and the bright portion of the stripe glittered as he bent over the contents of the folder. Finally he looked up, took one more bite of his sandwich, chewed and swallowed it, and then said—

"You're interested in the red-and-gold satin gay nineties #33-478, size ten. On the morning of the thirty-first of October last, we received a call for this costume with notice that it would be picked up before noon. Purcell, a man who quit us a week later to go into the army, handled the order. It was checked out"—Osborne leaned nearer to the folder and squinted at the order sheet—"A.M. That's as close as we signify these things. The rental price is for a full twenty-four-hour day no matter what time the merchandise is picked up."

"Who picked it up?" Ty asked.

"Mary Brownlee," Osborne said.

Mary Brownlee. Ty's mind fled back to the trial testimony. The drug store was at least a mile distant from this spot and Mary's absences from work were well accounted for on the morning of the 31st.

"That isn't possible," Ty said.

"It's on the pick-up sheet," Osborne answered.

"And your man—what was his name, Purcell? He's in the army."

Osborne nodded, and the light danced in stripes on his head.

"He's in the army," he said, "but I'm sitting here in my chair, Mr. Leander, just the way I was sitting on the morning of the thirty-first. I was drinking my coffee—no time for a sandwich because Halloween is such a busy day, and Purcell came in to show me the costume before he boxed it to take out. That's what isn't here in the folder. That's what Miss Sullavan thought you would want to know. That's why she sent you in to see me, Mr. Leander. I was sitting here, and Purcell came in to verify the costume. It had to be just like the one Julie San Martin wore in the picture—that was the stipulation on the phone order. I've got a photograph—full color, autographed."

Osborne moved some of the papers on the desk until he could reach a framed photo. He turned it about to face Ty. It was Julie in the costume. "With gratitude to Leon—"

"Wonderful woman," Osborne said, sadly. "Wonderful, but that's not what you've come to hear. . . . I checked out the costume and Purcell went back out to the customer. About that time, I swung my chair around—" Osborne illustrated his words with action. The chair pivoted until he was almost directly facing the windows. "I think it was a telephone call," he said. "I think I got a telephone call right after I talked to Purcell, and talking, you know how it is, I swung the chair around. Then I saw it—parked out at the curb. I couldn't miss it. I've got an Alfa Romeo myself. Sports car crazy, my wife says. An Alfa Romeo and before that a Karman Ghia—but a Ferrari I never quite made yet."

"A Ferrari!" Ty said.

Osborne gazed out as if the car were still visible.

"A beauty. A dream. My teen-age daughter would say, 'the utmost.' Bronze, Mr. Leander. All irridescent bronze."

He brought the chair around to face the desk again.

"Then I had to take a note on what the customer on the telephone was saying, so I swung around this way again.

"Next time I looked out, the Ferrari was gone. It so happened at that time, maybe because of being in the morning —oh, eleven o'clock, maybe, there was no other car out there. Now maybe Mary Brownlee called for that costume in a Ferrari. It was a hardtop model and I couldn't see inside. What do you think, Mr. Leander?"

Mary Brownlee hadn't called for a costume. Ty was positive of that. Julie—Julie's car and Julie. It had to be. What other answer was possible?

But Mr. Osborne had asked a question. Ty gave it back to him.

"What do you think?" he asked.

Osborne shook his head.

"I don't speculate on trials. I handle costumes. Maybe Mary Brownlee had a boy friend who drove a Ferrari. Maybe Mike Flanders killed her because of that; maybe he didn't. Have you heard the newscasts today, Mr. Leander?"

Ty hadn't heard, and he was almost afraid to ask what Osborne had heard. But it was only about Jorgensen, Flanders' missing witness, who had been found dead.

"Interesting," Osborne opined, "but I don't speculate. I don't ask questions. I'm in the costuming business. I won't even speculate as to why you came in here today, Mr. Leander. You ask questions and I answer them, that's all. I don't mix in anything. I don't want to offend anybody. Business isn't that good so I can offend anybody."

Ty had what he'd come for; still, he hesitated.

"You're very obliging, Mr. Osborne," he said. "You don't ask questions, but you answer then very well. Almost as if you had had a rehearsal."

Osborne looked up, smiling.

"This isn't the first time I answered them," he said.

"The police?" Ty asked.

"No. I guess the police are too sure of their man. They haven't bothered me. But Flanders' lawyer, Mr. Riley, he was here. He was here right after he took the case. I thought of that today when I heard about this second killing. Mark my word, Riley's got something up his sleeve."

"That's possible," Ty said moving away. "That's very possible."

Ty left the costuming house and returned to the station wagon. The day of the Mary Brownlee murder was beginning to fill in. The Ferrari. Alex had told him that Julie used it to drive her to a wallpaper house on Wilshire. That would have put them in the vicinity of the costumers' at the right time; but Alex hadn't said anything about this stop. On the contrary, she'd denied there was any connection between Mary's costume and her death. Either Alex had deliberately lied, or she didn't know what had happened.

He drove to Wilshire and turned east. He drove slowly, hoping to find the wallpaper house, until he sighted the drug store where Mary Brownlee had worked. He turned in at the parking lot, parked, and went inside. He went directly to the telephone booths and began to search the yellow book for wallpaper houses, and then his attention wandered to the conversation in progress at the counter.

Pearl Agnew, the waitress who had testified about Mary's fixation for Julie, was on duty. The trial had given her a brief glory, and she was taking full advantage of it. Her words were unimportant; but the sound of her voice reminded Ty of what she had said on the stand. Mary had boasted of knowing Julie. Pearl Agnew considered this blatant bragging; but now, after his talk with Mr. Osborne, it seemed not only possible but positive. And then Ty realized that he was standing beside the same telephone booth in which Mary Brownlee had made an important call on the morning of her death. A call to whom? To Julie? That wasn't possible. At the time of Mary's call, the house in the canyon had been empty—Julie had gone to Alex and he was on his way to the desert. To Cole? Cole, who had claimed a body from the morgue prior to the arrest of its accused murderer. Who else could she have called? Dana, who showed such an extraordinary interest in the case? Pearl Agnew's voice faded in the back of his mind as Ty groped for an answer that seemed at the very edge of consciousness. He raised his head and stared across the aisle from the booths, his mind barely registering what his eyes hardly saw. Cole, Dana, Alex, Marcus. Mary Brownlee had called someone—was it one of these? What had she said in the call? Had she told someone that she was drawing her money out of the bank and buying a ticket to Amarillo? If she had, was that the reason she was dead?

The answer gnawed at Ty's brain. Something seen and not recognized; something heard and not quite remembered. And then his eyes finally focused on what they had been staring at for some minutes. He lowered the telephone book and let it slip from his hands to dangle from the end of the anchoring chain, and moved across the aisle. The clerk, who had been stacking boxes the previous day, had rounded off his display with one demonstration toy typewriter, unboxed and equipped with a sheet of paper. The paper was already half-filled with the meaningless messages of curious customers, and now Ty saw what he had been searching for so long. He poked into his pocket for one of the letters, found it, and compared it to the typewritten sheet. The printing was the same.

And so it was Mary Brownlee who had written the letters. Why? Blackmail? No, these weren't blackmail letters; these were letters deliberately designed to break up a marriage. Hadn't he felt the tension coming on for months? Take two explosive temperaments, add concern over one ascending and one descending career, and then savor with a dash of rumor and malice. Mary Brownlee had written the letters. For money? Of course. But whose money? Who most wanted to destroy a marriage?

The answer was coming closer. Put pieces of time together. Compile scenes and scraps of words. Julie knew the answer. Julie coming through the confusion in his mind, trying to tell him the answer, trying to make him see. . . . Ty walked slowly away from the counter back to the parking lot. The wallpaper house was forgotten now; something else had taken precedent. He moved outside and stood beside the station wagon. Mary Brownlee had quarreled with Flanders on the night prior to her death. On the following morning, she had made a telephone call and then gone to the bank. Later, she had made a reservation on a plane to Amarillo. . . . A piece of an old newspaper blew against Ty's leg. He kicked it aside and it went dancing across the parking lot. Windy weather. Bad weather for fire watchers in the canyon. Ty watched the paper skip and whirl until it disappeared beneath one of the cars, and it reminded him of the way canyon fires skip and leap, destroying one side of the road and leaving the other untouched.

Or destroying one section of a house and leaving the other section whole. . . .

Yes, Julie. I'm beginning to see. It was a round trip to Amarillo; not one way, as intended. That means only one thing, doesn't it? That can mean only one thing.

The back road to the house had been open. Ty's mind worked at the thought until it came clear. The return trip from Amarillo had been made on the day the canyon fire began—the day after Michael Flanders had been charged with murder . . . and the back road had been open. Emerald ear clips—that was the next thing. Julie was careless with fine things. They would have been in the jewel box in her dressing room. But the bluie dress and the orange dress and the overnight bag—where had they been?

A murderer leaves a confession behind. Ty remembered his own words. He got back inside the station wagon, no longer interested in the mission he'd begun. He had a long drive ahead of him to find the answer he already knew. . . .

Downtown, Lieutenant Janus was making a point.

"You see the hammer," he said. "A good hammer; but not too frequently used to judge by the appearance of it. Not something out of a carpenter's tool box, would you say, Mr. Riley?"

"It might be," Cole answered. "Even a carpenter buys a new hammer occasionally."

"But this isn't a new hammer. See—there's rust on one of the claws. It's just a hammer that hasn't been used a great deal—to hang a picture, perhaps, or to pound a tire iron into place."

"Imagination," Cole said, "not evidence."

"No, not evidence," Janus admitted. "I'm aware of that, Mr. Riley. I'm aware of something else, too. This hammer has a manufacturer's name stamped on it. We give this name to a man and he checks the stores in which it is sold. We check with the manufacturer to get the year in which it was made. We trace and we track, Mr. Riley. It takes time; but we'll finally find its purchaser. Of course, that may not be necessary. That's the hard way. We took prints off this hammer. They're being checked now. I don't have to tell you whose prints we're checking, do I?"

Cole didn't answer.

"Use your head, Mr. Riley. You're an intelligent man. Leander is a close friend—you've known him for years. You've been in his home—probably driven his car. Have you ever seen this hammer before?"

Cole smiled tightly.

"You're an intelligent man, Lieutenant," he said. "I've already told you—I'm Mr. Leander's legal representative. I don't even know what a hammer looks like."

"All right," Janus said. "I was just trying to avoid publicity."

"Give me a few hours," Cole said.

"Why, Mr. Riley?"

"To locate Mr. Leander. To get his story."

"And coach him in an alibi?"

"I don't think he needs an alibi. I think he needs help."

Lieutenant Janus was a patient man. He put down the hammer and turned to Cole with tired eyes.

"Do you realize what we've got on Leander?" he said. "First the suicide attempt—"

"That was a stunt," Cole insisted. "A deliberate stunt."

"You didn't tell me that before."

"No, I didn't. I thought Ty would sober up and abandon the idea. Apparently he hasn't. He set out to convict himself of Flanders' crime." Incredulity crept into Janus' eyes. Cole, noticing, continued. "That's what he told us. He didn't want to live any more, and so he decided to strike back at the world he was sick of by proving himself guilty of Flanders' crime."

"Are you serious, Mr. Riley?" Janus demanded.

"I am. The question is—is he?"

Janus glanced down at the hammer again. The scowl on his face had settled down to stay.

"Jorgensen's dead—and that's serious," he said grimly. "Why didn't you tell me that story before?"

"I didn't think you'd believe it," Cole said.

"Do you?"

Cole hesitated. He'd followed Janus all morning—the Alvarado Street Hotel, Ekberg's home, Alex's, the rooming house—Ty had to be somewhere; but he wasn't going to be found by a man searching for him in a black-and-white prowl car. Cole was anxious to get away; but when he looked up, Janus's question was still in his eyes.

"I don't know," Cole said. "At this moment, I actually don't know."

Janus continued to stare at him. "Mary Brown," he said. "You heard Ekberg's conversation just before you intercepted his call to Leander. Mary Brown returned, via Southwestern, to International Airport . . ." Janus paused. He'd glimpsed something in Cole's face that shouldn't have been there. "What do you know about that, Mr. Riley?"

"Nothing," Cole said tightly.

"Who is Mary Brown?"

"I don't know, Lieutenant."

"And if you did, you wouldn't tell us—is that right?" Janus' hand reached out and took up the telephone from his desk. "Keenan," he said, "find out all you can about Mary Brown, a passenger on Southwestern Airlines coming into International Airport on December second. No, I don't know where from—that's what I want you to find out. Where from, where to, and why." He replaced the phone in the cradle and looked up at Cole. "December second," he repeated. "Does that date mean anything to you, Mr. Riley?"

It meant a fire raging in Malibu Canyon. It meant newspaper stories and television coverage. It meant blocked roads and a stream of canyon residents scurrying for safety. It meant a house burning—

Cole turned toward the door.

"Mr. Riley."

He paused long enough to hear Janus's promise.

"I'll give you two hours. If you're not back in this office with Leander by that time, I'm turning everything loose to get him."

It was a long ride from Mrs. Herbert's rooming house to Alex's hilltop perch. The taxi meter ground merrily; but Marcus fretted restlessly with the creases of his trousers. Elderly, lonely women did see and hear things of great interest. Marcus' face was grave. On the seat beside him was the latest edition of the paper carrying the full story of Cappy Jorgensen's death. He had read it and folded the paper again. There was nothing in the story—nothing important. The press knew only what they had been told, and Marcus could only wonder about whatever they had not been told.

At the end of the driveway, Marcus alighted and dismissed the cab. The gesture was automatic. Not until the cab was gone did he consider the fact that Alex's Lincoln was missing from the garage. He entered the building and started toward the stairway to the inner entrance—then paused, his attention arrested by a fading spot on the cement. He moved closer and stood for a moment looking down at his discovery. It appeared to be crankcase drippings that had been scrubbed in a partially successful attempt at removal; but the spot wasn't in the area where Alex usually kept the Lincoln. It was in the area where she had kept the furniture.

Staring at the spot on the floor solved no problems. Marcus turned away and went to the stairs. At the top of the stairs, he tried the door. It was locked. By this time, it was obvious that Alex was gone. He left the garage and followed the path back to Dana's studio. Dana's Ford was in the garage—as usual, the studio was open. Marcus let himself in. The wind had blown up a ceiling of clouds to leaden the skylight and the unlighted room, at late afternoon, had a stark coldness that even the flamboyant cushions couldn't relieve. And the room was empty. Dana and Alex—both gone. Marcus was tired. Wringing a story out of Mrs. Herbert had required tact and charm, and Marcus loathed both. He looked about hopefully, located a small liquor cabinet, and was pouring himself a glass of cognac when his eyes discovered a more than usual untidiness on the floor. He left the drink untouched and went to investigate. Newspapers. Dana's careful collection of newspapers were scattered and torn. They seemed to add to the general air of desolation and abandonment. Marcus stood and stared down at them for some minutes, and then, making the decision reluctantly, went to the telephone.

Chapter Seventeen

A murderer leaves a confession behind. The thought was a spur at the mind. Ty drove rapidly. The afternoon was waning, and he needed light for what he had to do. The canyon was a black-patched tunnel through which the wind probed relentlessly. Black stubble couldn't bow before it, but there were wide patches on either side of the road that had been untouched by flame, and it was this that urged Ty on. A canyon fire was unpredictable. One house might be destroyed—the next one untouched. But one house had been destroyed—one wing of it—completely. With all his searching, Ty had only now realized the most important of all clues had been overlooked.

He by-passed the village and took a cut-off to the back road approach. There was something he had to see: trees, shrubbery, dry brown grass untouched by fire. The passage had been clear. He approached the house from above for the first time since the fire, and looked down on a phenomenon not noticeable from any other plane. The charred skeleton of the ruined portion stood within a small black circle of destruction. No path of approach was visible, and the nearest burned area was an opposite hillside at least two hundred yards away. With a strong wind behind it, a fire could leap that distance—but had it? Ty drove slowly. The roof of the stone portion came into view—not a shingle blackened. None of the shrubs around the house had been touched; nothing was burned but that frame portion. Slowly, it disappeared from view behind the rocky slope that led up to the road, and then Ty applied the brakes and brought the station wagon to a sudden halt. Just short of the entrance to the driveway a car was parked on the shoulder—Alex's Lincoln. He paused long enough to make certain of that and then drove on and turned in at the driveway. The drive sloped sharply downward. Now he noticed the trees and shrubbery—green, untouched by fire. He parked before the garage and unlocked the door. The Ferrari was inside. Julie had never used the trunk. Except for the spare and the tire equipment, it was empty. He went then to the shelves at the end of the garage and began to search; but there was nothing of interest there. He went upstairs.

"Alex—"

At the top of the stairs, he called out. There was no answer. He went to Julie's room. Nothing had been touched; nothing was any different than it had been in the morning. He checked the closet. The blue and orange dresses were still there. He returned to the hall and proceeded to the doorway to the patio stairway—a stairway now burned away. He stood for a moment staring out at the charred fragments as if they could give him a story—and then, from somewhere in the ravine below, he heard a sharp cry.

"Alex—"

The ravine ran deep, and was lined with scrub growth. He could see nothing from above. He began to clamber down the slope, suddenly aware that the ravine was the place to search for his answer. At the bottom of the ravine, he turned toward the direction of the sound and then broke into running when it was followed by a shot.

A few yards ahead, behind a clump of twisted shrubs, he found Alex. She wasn't alone. At her feet—the gun beside him—was Dana. Ty dropped to his knees. The wound on Dana's chest was neat and deadly. There had been one shot, and that one instantly fatal. Ty looked up. Alex's face was white.

"He made me come," she said.

"Dana made you?" Ty echoed.

"The gun—it's his."

"But why?" Ty demanded.

"He did it," Alex said. "He did it all. There—"

She seemed to be in a state of shock. Ty followed the direction in which she pointed, and then his eyes found what he'd come to find. Half-hidden behind one of the rocks was a battered kerosene can.

"He did it," Alex repeated. "Ty, believe me—"

Ty left Dana's body and went to the kerosene can. He didn't have to touch it to know that it was empty. He turned and looked toward the charred ruins of the house, and then his eyes found Alex's. They were searching his face for response.

"I found an oil stain on the floor of the garage," she said. "Dana discovered me there."

"An oil stain?" Ty echoed.

"Where he kept Julie's Ferrari—behind the sets."

Ty stared at her. Her hair was wild in the wind; her face drawn.

"What are you talking about?" he demanded.

"He killed her," Alex said. "He had the acid in his studio."

"Who did he kill? Julie?"

Alex hesitated. Anger was overtaking the shock on Ty's face. She measured it carefully and said—

"Yes, Ty. Julie. Julie and Mary Brownlee. Julie first on Halloween night."

"But why?"

"Because of those letters—those awful letters he'd hired Mary to write hoping to break up your marriage. Dana was in love with Julie, Ty. Didn't you know that? He was in love with her and he hated you. He hired Mary to write the letters so they could never be traced to him, or the machine they were written with found in the house. You know how we're all in and out of it all the time. But Mary was having trouble with her boy friend and wanted to leave town. Dana wouldn't let her—not after Julie left you to come to me. Everything he'd planned was working out. He couldn't let Mary leave then. That's why he promised her Julie's costume for the party if she'd stay. He knew how vain she was about her resemblance to Julie. Ty— No, Ty. Don't!"

Ty had taken a step forward. His foot kicked the gun on the ground. He stooped and picked it up.

"The fingerprints—"

There was fear in Alex's eyes; but he ignored the warning. He held the gun in his hand.

"How did he kill Julie?" Ty demanded.

"How?" she repeated.

"How did he kill Julie?"

"It was because of the telephone call," Alex said. "The call Mary Brownlee made after her quarrel with Flanders at the Halloween party. He'd threatened her again and she had a plane ticket to Amarillo. She'd bought it earlier in the day after her first call to Dana—the one that sent him to the costumers' for a costume like Julie's. She was still undecided, even after he made her promise to stay on. But that night—"

"Halloween night?"

"—Halloween night, after the party, she was too afraid to stay in the city any longer. She called Dana to tell him she was going and Julie—Julie had gone to Dana's studio."

"Why?" Ty asked.

"I don't know why. I only know what Dana told me. She was there when the call came, she heard . . ."

Alex's face was deathly white. Never had the skin looked so tight. It seemed barely to stretch over the bones.

"And so Dana had to kill Julie—is that it?" Ty said.

"They quarreled. It was an accident. She fell."

"And then he took her to Mary's apartment."

"Yes. He called Mary back first and told her it was all right for her to go if she would leave the outer door to the rooming house open so he could drive by and pick up the costume. Then he drove over with Julie's body and the acid—"

"And Mary Brownlee was already gone."

"Yes."

"And it was after ten—Gruenther's hearing aid was turned off and the light's dim in that lower hall. But Mary Brownlee returned."

"After she heard that Flanders had been charged with murder," Alex said. "Her murder."

"I thought she hated Flanders."

"Not hate, Ty. She was afraid of him, but she didn't hate him. She loved him. Women love in strange ways. She came back to save him, and so Dana had to kill her, too. He gave her a drink with poison in it—there are several poisons among the chemicals in the studio. He wanted Flanders to be found guilty."

"And the fire had broken out in the canyon," Ty mused.

"Yes. It was on television and in all of the papers. Dana killed Mary and drove her body out here, taking the back road. The newscasts gave all the details of how the fire was progressing. He wasn't sure that it would reach your house, so he brought the can of kerosene to make certain. That's why he brought me out here—to help him search for the can. He knew you were on his trail. You mentioned the emerald ear clips, don't you remember? He must have been frightened then because he had taken the clips from Julie's room and replaced them on Mary's body. And the dresses—you mentioned them. Dana had them. He'd driven the Ferrari out the night after Julie's murder—as soon as he'd had a chance to come out and find your note. He walked back to the highway and hitched a ride to the Palisades. But he didn't return the dresses and the bag because he wanted you, and the police, to think she had run away from you. Mary wasn't dead then. There was no one to take Julie's place. He had to bring the dresses and bag out this morning."

Alex paused. She had spoken rapidly, her poise shattered by that body in the gully behind them. She looked gaunt and haggard and tall as a shaft in a shapeless tweed coat, the tails of which wind-whipped the legs of her narrow trousers. On her feet were the same soft-soled shoes she had been wearing when she arrived at Dana's studio in the morning. The hood of Dana's Ford had been warm, but there was this that Ty remembered about Alex—those soft-soled shoes.

"What about Cappy Jorgensen?" he asked.

"Dana killed him, too. He followed you, Ty. He knew about that hotel on Alvarado Street—he'd been looking for Jorgensen, too. He followed your station wagon and parked behind you in the fog. He took your hammer from the glove compartment. He went on through the back door of the bar and waited until you had gone out, and then called Jorgensen out into the alley and killed him. He had to destroy Flanders' alibi. Killing once makes it easier the second and third times."

"And the fourth?" Ty asked.

For a few seconds, the wind played between them, scurrying up dust and dry leaves. The wind that Alex didn't like. Alex stared at the gun in his hand.

"I had to kill Dana," she insisted. "He was going to kill me because I'd found him out. He wouldn't have told me all those things if he hadn't intended to kill me. I knew that Flanders is innocent."

"Yes," Ty said. "I've known that for several weeks."

"Then you knew that Julie had been murdered?"

The answer was difficult; but it had lain in the back of his mind all these weeks. Behind the hope that the body in the ruins had been that of a stranger, and the body in Mary Brownlee's room had really been Mary Brownlee, was a certain knowing that came of Julie's voice whispering in his mind. The dead sing softly. The dead sing true.

"Yes," Ty said, "I knew that, too."

"Then that suicide attempt and the story of wanting to

convict yourself for Flanders' crime were false?"

"From the beginning," Ty said. "I've played the frenetic writer from the beginning for just one reason, Alex. Just one reason. I was determined to come face to face with Julie's murderer."

Dana's body was sprawled on the ground a few yards behind him, but Ty didn't turn.

"Why did you send Mary Brownlee to Amarillo?" he asked.

Alex said nothing.

And then, suddenly, it was six years ago in Alex's studio in New York. They had all come for cocktails—Marcus, Cole, Julie and himself. The sky was a wild gray, and the rain washed down against the skylight in a driving torrent. The grayness seemed to permeate the room, in spite of the gaiety of the occasion. And the occasion was Ty's announcement of his impending marriage to Julie. It had come as a shock to them all; but it was Alex who had accidentally toppled a stone cat from its pedestal and narrowly missed Julie's foot.

Julie had laughed.

"If I'm ever murdered," she'd said, "you'll know who hated me."

Julie had been joking; but the remembered glimpse of Alex's face had no merriment in it. And then Alex had said—

"It's this damned panhandle wind. My nerves go to pieces in a wind. . . ."

Six years ago.

Now Alex began to answer. "Dana—" she said.

"No, not Dana. He wasn't there." Alex didn't know what he was talking about. He had to find other reasons. "Dana wasn't with Julie when the Ferrari was parked in front of the costumers', was he? But you were. You went inside and picked up the costume you had ordered in Mary Brownlee's name right after that long, frantic call she put in from the drug store. You told me the truth about one thing: the letters from Mary couldn't stop then—not with Julie under your own roof, evidence that your plan to separate us was working."

"No, Ty—" Alex said.

"Yes, Alex. Remember, Dana wasn't with me at the bar when the bellboy brought the message from the travel

159

desk; but you were. You knew then that I was on the track of that flight to Amarillo. Why Amarillo? Mary Brownlee, very likely, had never been outside the city in her life; and yet she chose Amarillo for her hiding place. I'd forgotten where you were from. But you must have talked about it to Mary. The past of a successful woman who hob-nobs with glamour would have fascinated her. When she felt like running, she ran to the one place you'd given her."

"Ty—please! I told you everything!"

"Everything but the truth. It was you, Alex—not Dana. It was you who knew about the hotel on Alvarado Street. It was you who followed me to Long Beach and took the hammer from my car. In fact, now that I remember, it was you who gave me the hammer when the house was completed. A gift of the builder, you said."

All of the lies had been answered. There was nothing left but the truth of the few feet between them and the gun in Ty's hand. But now there was a sound above them—a car in the driveway, a door slamming, voices rising.

"Leander—are you here? Leander—"

It was Janus. Ty glanced up and saw him come around the corner of the studio. He paused at the edge of the ravine, looking down. As yet, he hadn't seen them. He wasn't alone. Cole was with him.

There was little time left; but Alex didn't seem afraid. She only seemed bewildered that he didn't understand.

"It was an accident," she said. "You must believe me, Ty, it was an accident. Julie was in the guest room when Mary called me after her quarrel with Flanders at the Halloween party. She answered the extension, thinking it might be you. She heard Mary talk about the letters she'd written for me—I knew that when I heard the extension click. I started for her room, but we met in the hall at the head of the stairs. You know Julie's temper. She began screaming at me and flailing with her hands—I had to fight her in self-defense. She fell, Ty. She fell down the stairs and struck her head on the lion. It was an accident, but I was glad for you. She was ruining you, Ty. She was killing your gift—"

Her words ran together in hopeless confusion. If she had tried to run, he would have fired. But she stood pleading with him to understand the great benefit she had done him, and hatred turned to pity. Women did love in strange ways.

And so he waited for Janus and Cole, not even needing a gun to hold her.

Later, in his office downtown, Lieutenant Janus filled in the details.

"It was Mr. Anatole who called me," he explained. "He was at the Draeger home and it was empty. He did some very fast thinking. His mind was running in the same direction as yours, Mr. Leander; but he had a less vigorous and less dangerous method. He questioned Mrs. Herbert."

"That sounds like Marcus," Ty said. "Get the audience reaction."

"It was a good idea. Under prompting, she admitted having heard Mr. Riley's voice in Mary Brownlee's apartment some months before her death."

"Cole? Why? What for?"

"For Julie," Cole said. "Mary Brownlee had tried to turn her resemblance to Julie into profit via the forgery route. She was caught, but it was a first offense. Julie's heart was always too big for her judgment. She refused to bring charges."

"Did Alex know that?" Ty asked.

"She knew. She even went around to the rooming house with me one day when we we're getting Mary rehabilitated."

"That was the beginning of her plan," Janus added, "although she may not have realized it at the time. But the seed was there. All it needed was time to grow. When Mr. Anatole called me, I got in touch with Cole Riley. He admitted that Miss Draeger knew about Mary Brownlee. By that time we both knew about that two-way flight to Amarillo, and Mr. Riley explained that Miss Draeger had come from that area. There had to be some connection."

"Janus suggested going to the ruins of your house in the canyon," Cole added. "He said it was a hunch. I think he's psychic."

"Just an old professional cop," Janus said. "I wanted another look at the ruins. The story Riley told me after I checked on that Amarillo flight we heard Ekberg mention in his call to you blew the Flanders' case wide open."

"Story?" Ty echoed. "What story?"

"A wild story," Cole confessed. "I realize that now; but in the pre-dawn hours of the morning after what was to be known as the Mary Brownlee murder, it sounded convincing. Alex called me. She was in a state of near hysteria—no tears, but that terrible tension I've often known her to have. I drove out to her house, and what she told me caused me to take the course of action I did take—claiming Mary's body and defending Mike Flanders.

"The version of what had occurred that she gave me then was quite different from the truth Ty forced from her a few hours ago," Cole continued. "It was similar only in that Julie had interrupted a call to Alex from Mary. According to Alex, Mary had pulled her old forgery act again and was in trouble. Alex had taken an interest in her at the time of the first forgery, and she turned to her for help. Now we all know that Julie had a generous nature; but, like most generous people, she became enraged when anyone took advantage of her generosity. After hearing that telephone conversation, she rushed from the house. Apparently, she raced back to Dana's studio, took the acid because, when Alex dressed and followed her to Mary's apartment, Mary was already dead and disfigured."

"And you believed that story?" Ty demanded.

"At four o'clock in the morning," Cole said, "with Alex's nerves as taut as a bowstring and in full knowledge of Julie's temperament—yes, I believed it. I had no reason not to believe it. I'd seen Julie at Alex's a few hours earlier for cocktails; I knew how terribly upset she was. I didn't know, naturally, about those tormenting letters. But I did know Mary Brownlee. Unlike Julie, I never trusted her. It wasn't at all difficult to believe that she had needled Julie at the wrong time with disastrous results. It happens all the time—ask any lawyer. That's why we have so many pleas of temporary insanity."

"The eye of the hurricane," Ty said.

"Exactly. And so I had to believe Alex—I was afraid not to. Julie was gone; we didn't know where. It never occurred to me to search Alex's garage for the Ferrari. I went into action. When no one came forward to claim Mary Brownlee's body, I did so. My reason, if anyone asked, was based on our slight acquaintance at the time of the forgery. I watched for any break in the case while we waited for Julie to return. Flanders was arrested. I took over his defense for two reasons. In the first place, I knew he was innocent and wanted to save his life. In the second, I wanted to be on top of what might develop during the course of the trial and not under it. Then the fire broke out in the canyon and what I, along with the rest of the world, believed to be Julie's body was found in the ruins. Her car was in the garage. It was natural to assume that she had returned from her hiding place and been trapped in the blaze. Julie was dead. I believed that. All I could do for Flanders was fight for his life."

"You might have told your story to the D.A.," Janus suggested.

"And backed it up with what? I hadn't a shred of evidence—only Alex's story. There was no reason to doubt that until this morning when I learned of Cappy Jorgensen's death. What's more important, I was still trying to protect Julie. Julie dead was quite different from Julie a murderess. Everything I've done was to protect Julie—not myself, Ty. That's what you thought, wasn't it? I was the murderer you were stalking. That's why you invited me to your carefully staged suicide scene."

Ty's face was tired and haggard. He hadn't shaved all day, and his beard came in heavy. But he wasn't as haggard as he had been two days ago. Something he had been searching for was found.

"Yes," he admitted, "I was stalking you—up until I learned that Julie's car had been parked in front of the costumers' on the morning of the murder. Julie and Alex had gone out together that morning—Alex told me that; but she didn't mention the costumers', and yet, if Julie dropped Alex off before going to Nick's station at eleven-thirty, and if the Ferrari had been seen at the costumers' at eleven, it just wasn't possible for Alex not to have known of that shop. Yet, when I'd asked her about the costume yesterday afternoon, she said nothing about it."

Janus nodded. "You were right. Miss Draeger was in the car. It's all in her confession. She bribed Mary Brownlee to stay on by getting her the costume—just as she claimed Dana Quist had done. She then told your wife, on the way

to the wallpaper showing, that she must pick up a Halloween costume for a friend. She didn't identify the friend, and
your wife, having never been to the rooming house, suspected nothing when she was asked to call for Miss Draeger
at that address."

"It still took me a little while to put all of the pieces together," Ty added, "there were so many of them. It began
with an oil change sticker and a mileage reading which led
me to Nick's and put Julie's car in front of the rooming
house at a little past noon on the day of the murder. Of
course I suspected you, Cole. You were defending Flanders
on the flimsiest of excuses. There had to be some real reason. Julie's bag and dresses were missing. She hadn't
driven but forty miles. There was a striking resemblance between Julie and the dead girl. I tried to fight down my suspicion; but I couldn't. I had to know why Julie had gone to
that rooming house. I had to know why the woman found
dead in that room was wearing a costume exactly like one
Julie had worn in a film, and why her face had been destroyed with acid. I had that much to go on when I took
Mary Brownlee's room and made my play for the headlines. I hoped the police would help me find what I knew
was wrong."

"You might have told us," Janus suggested.

"I did tell you—in my way. In the only way I could grab
attention away from Flanders. I aroused your curiosity."

"And nearly got yourself arrested as a murder suspect."

"I think that was a scare play," Ty said. "Alex had given
me the hammer—it couldn't be traced to me. But she knew
it was in my car, and she knew that Jorgensen had to be si-
lenced or Flanders' alibi would be established. That was
when I really suspected you, Cole—when I found Cappy
Jorgensen's body in the fog. But that didn't add up with
what I learned today—or with what Julie was trying to tell
me from the beginning."

Cole and Janus looked at him strangely, and Ty smiled for
the first time in more than a month.

"No, I'm not going off again—actually or faked," he said.
"It may sound strange, but all along, ever since I returned,
it's as if I had been looking for Julie—and finding her. The
answer had to go back to those letters I found in her desk.

They were an act of malice. Malice and acid go together, don't they?"

"I once arrested a very pious mother," Janus recalled, "who had killed and dismembered her daughter-in-law in the basement, and then transported the remains to the desert in a garbage can concealed in the trunk of her car—and all because she was convinced the girl was ruining her son's career."

"But Julie was so small," Ty said, quietly. "Alex was so strong and Julie was so small."

"Looking for Julie and finding her, you said," Cole reminded.

And that was true. Julie's song was a lie—every word of it.

"Yes," Ty answered, "—inside of me. Alive."

BLACK LIZARD BOOKS

JIM THOMPSON
- *AFTER DARK, MY SWEET* $3.95
- *THE ALCOHOLICS* $3.95
- *THE CRIMINAL* $3.95
- *CROPPER'S CABIN* $3.95
- *THE GETAWAY* $3.95
- *THE GRIFTERS* $3.95
- *A HELL OF A WOMAN* $3.95
- *NOTHING MORE THAN MURDER* $3.95
- *POP. 1280* $3.95
- *RECOIL* $3.95
- *SAVAGE NIGHT* $3.95
- *A SWELL LOOKING BABE* $3.95
- *WILD TOWN* $3.95

HARRY WHITTINGTON
- *THE DEVIL WEARS WINGS* $3.95
- *FIRES THAT DESTROY* $4.95
- *FORGIVE ME, KILLER* $3.95
- *A MOMENT TO PREY* $4.95
- *A TICKET TO HELL* $3.95
- *WEB OF MURDER* $3.95

CHARLES WILLEFORD
- *THE BURNT ORANGE HERESY* $3.95
- *COCKFIGHTER* $3.95
- *PICK-UP* $3.95

ROBERT EDMOND ALTER
- *CARNY KILL* $3.95
- *SWAMP SISTER* $3.95

W.L. HEATH
- *ILL WIND* $3.95
- *VIOLENT SATURDAY* $3.95

PAUL CAIN
- *FAST ONE* $3.95
- *SEVEN SLAYERS* $3.95

FREDRIC BROWN
- *HIS NAME WAS DEATH* $3.95
- *THE FAR CRY* $3.95

DAVID GOODIS
- *BLACK FRIDAY* $3.95
- *CASSIDY'S GIRL* $3.95
- *NIGHTFALL* $3.95
- *SHOOT THE PIANO PLAYER* $3.95
- *STREET OF NO RETURN* $3.95

HELEN NIELSEN
- *DETOUR* $4.95
- *SING ME A MURDER* $4.95

DAN J. MARLOWE
- *THE NAME OF THE GAME IS DEATH* $4.95
- *NEVER LIVE TWICE* $4.95

MURRAY SINCLAIR
- *ONLY IN L.A.* $4.95
- *TOUGH LUCK L.A.* $4.95

AND OTHERS . . .
- **FRANCIS CARCO** • *PERVERSITY* $3.95
- **BARRY GIFFORD** • *PORT TROPIQUE* $3.95
- **NJAMI SIMON** • *COFFIN & CO.* $3.95
- **ERIC KNIGHT (RICHARD HALLAS)** • *YOU PLAY THE BLACK AND THE RED COMES UP* $3.95
- **GERTRUDE STEIN** • *BLOOD ON THE DINING ROOM FLOOR* $6.95
- **KENT NELSON** • *THE STRAIGHT MAN* $3.50
- **JIM NISBET** • *THE DAMNED DON'T DIE* $3.95
- **STEVE FISHER** • *I WAKE UP SCREAMING* $4.95
- **LIONEL WHITE** • *THE KILLING* $4.95
- *THE BLACK LIZARD ANTHOLOGY OF CRIME FICTION* Edited by **EDWARD GORMAN** $8.95

HARDCOVER ORIGINALS:
LETHAL INJECTION by **JIM NISBET** $15.95
GOODBYE L.A. by **MURRAY SINCLAIR** $15.95

Black Lizard Books are available at most bookstores or directly from the publisher. In addition to list price, please send $1.00/postage for the first book and $.50 for each additional book to **Black Lizard Books, 833 Bancroft Way, Berkeley, CA 94710.** California residents please include sales tax.